SLAUGHTER FIELDS

TRENCH RAIDERS BOOK 1

THOMAS WOOD

BOLEYNBENNETT PUBLISHING

Copyright © 2019 by Thomas Wood

All rights reserved.

No part of this book may be reproduced in any form or by any electronic or mechanical means, including information storage and retrieval systems, without written permission from the author, except for the use of brief quotations in a book review.

This book is a work of fiction. Names, characters, places, and incidents either are products of the author's imagination or are used fictitiously. Any resemblance to actual persons, living or dead, events, or locales is entirely coincidental.
Thomas Wood

Visit my website at www.ThomasWoodBooks.com

Printed in the United Kingdom

First Printing: January 2019
by
BoleynBennett Publishing

GRAB ANOTHER BOOK FOR FREE

If you enjoy this book, why not pick up another one, completely free?

'Enemy Held Territory' follows Special Operations Executive Agent, Maurice Dumont as he inspects the defences at the bridges at Ranville and Benouville. Fast paced and exciting, this Second World War thriller is one you won't want to miss!
Details can be found at the back of this book.

1

The first couple of stumbling steps that I had taken out into No Man's Land had been relatively easy. There had been no shell holes or machine gun fire that had tried to trip me up with their lethal darts, but just a deadly silence as the men of the 2nd Battalion uneasily crept their way over the top of the parapet.

Artillery had been pulverising this small little field for the best part of half an hour, so what had once been a lovely, furrowed and well-maintained farmer's field, was nothing more than a barren wasteland, stripped of anything that made it seem like it was planet earth.

Apart from the battalion as they inched closer to the Germans, nothing seemed to move; the ground had settled now, content not to be thrown around like a child's toy and no birds seemed to frequent the air, that was filled with acrid smoke and horrid fumes.

But the silence was quickly smashed to pieces by a tumultuous pandemonium, as if the world was trying to make up for the few seconds of silence that we had been granted half a second before. It all seemed to engulf me, seizing my body and everything within it, so much so that I could barely string a cohesive thought together as I stood there.

I looked across at the desolate and churned up mud that we would have to advance across, wondering how it was even remotely possible for anything to live in this kind of a world. Even the hardiest of creatures would struggle to survive out here, a meagre worm would need to fight to take sustenance from the contaminated soil and would more than likely be cut down by a raking machine gun himself.

In the distance, as our heads had gradually risen up and over the top of the sandbagged parapet, the faint booms of the retorting German artillery were just about audible, as if someone was gently tapping their fist into the palm of their hand, continuously.

I had expected to hear maybe four or five thumps in retaliation to our artillery, but instead the faint punches on the horizon continued to resound, right until the point when they were superseded by a far more arrogant and eminent crash, as the first of the rounds began to unsettle the disgruntled earth once again.

A curtain of dirt was immediately thrown up ahead of me, in the same way that a spurt of water would erupt from a garden hose that had been kinked for a long time, except the spurts of dirt continued for as far as I could see, both left and right. As soon as one cloud of dirt and dust pattered its way back to earth, another would take its place, as if each one had been given very specific instructions on where to land and when.

The shells that began to pulverise the ground before

us, seemed to act as some sort of a starter gun, as whistles began to shriek out across the fog, the bellows of terrified teenagers as they walked towards the enemy replying to the shrill screams.

"Come on then!" screamed one man, as he threw a leather football over the top of the trench, proceeding to drop kick it as far as he could, into the cloud of smoke that had appeared all around us.

The artillery shells knew of no let up, and continued to rain down on us heavier than a tonne of marbles being dropped from the sky.

"Let's go, boys!" hollered Lieutenant Fairweather, a young but driven individual, who had taken command of five platoon shortly before the rest of them had shipped out for France.

Screams of confidence suddenly erupted from everyone's lips, including mine, as we began to march along No Man's Land, as one. I felt immortal as I stood side by side to two of my comrades, weapons in hands and ready to see how much damage our artillery had done just minutes before. We were sure that the enemy would be completely decimated, as there was no way that anyone could have lived through the sheer hell that we had put them through, courtesy of the Royal Field Artillery and their eighteen pounders.

Without warning, some screams were simply shut off, as if the man who bellowed them had switched his own voice box off, in amongst all the excitement. It did not take me too long to work out why, as one shell suddenly spewed molten lead and bits of dirt in every possible direction, just over to my left, and I watched as one man's lower leg was ripped from his body, as he was sent cartwheeling through the air.

Every fibre of my being wanted to run over and help the man, who now lay screaming in a pitiful agony, as he clutched at the bloody stump that was now his leg.

"Don't think about it, Ellis! Keep moving!" I continued to stagger forward, my head turned backwards towards the screaming figure, as the gruff, curt tones of Sergeant Needs began to filter through into my mind.

"He's gone. Forget him."

He seemed so at home shouting that I found it surprising that he hadn't ruptured his vocal chords by now, his deep booming tones fighting off the competition that the artillery had to offer.

The continuous field of churned up and slightly sodden mud began to clump to the bottom of my boots and I could already feel the first few signs of leakage in my socks, as the coldness of the early morning began to bite gently at the very tips of my toes.

"Okay then lads, keep your heads."

We began to advance into the curtain of artillery that had been put on as a welcome for us, the confusion and chaos ratcheting up ten-fold as we did so.

As I marched ever closer to what I presumed would be my grisly end, I moved my right hand upwards until it just brushed over the breast pocket of my tunic. I rubbed it around the outline of the brassy object that was perched in there and tried to take as much comfort out of it as I possibly could.

I was not superstitious or ritualistic, but it did give me a boost, a confidence. And, failing that, I was hoping that it might protect the vital organ that was quivering behind it.

The screams of men were now as continuous and harrowing as the sound of the bullying artillery, as I watched body after body being thrown through the air, some with limbs cruelly severed from their housings, before they slumped to the ground.

I slid down into a shell hole, to try and catch my breath, drenching myself in a bath tub of rancid water as I did so. Trying to escape from the freezing clutches of the water, I scrabbled up the opposite side of the hole; the wet, compact mud, making it ever so slightly easier to do so than if it was bone dry.

I peeked out over the top of the hole, waiting for the next shell to burst, which took less than half a second. Yanking myself from the hole, I charged towards the falling mud, reasoning that two shells wouldn't hit the same place twice, no matter how hard it tried.

I knew that my thoughts were confused and childlike, but I wanted to stay alive and, right now, this seemed like my best possible prospect of doing so.

The men that had stood either side of me, the rest of five platoon, were nowhere to be seen, and I suddenly had the horrible feeling that I was out here all on my own, the rest of them being ordered to retreat without my knowledge. But, through the clouds of smoke, I could make out figures and supposed that I had been left behind, a prospect even worse than being out in No Man's Land on one's own.

Everything that could be on fire was; from the fallen and rotten branches that had been blasted from their roots weeks ago, to a small stone structure, that I assumed was once some sort of house, that seemed impossible to be ablaze.

Men trod over flames and bodies, as if they were merely stepping over a small twig on a Sunday afternoon stroll, as they defiantly strode towards the enemy trenches.

I jogged to catch up with the marching figures, the heavy weight of my kit throwing itself up and down and forcing me to slow my pace up to a more leisurely degree.

I got a coating of dirt splashed across my face as another shell exploded somewhere in front of me, blinding me for a moment as my body tried desperately to get rid of the flecks of dirt that sat on my eyeballs.

When I was able to see again, the little flashing lights that accompanied the rattling I had heard half a second before, began to light up all around me, as the sickening sound of bullets tearing through flesh and smacking into bones could be heard above the din of artillery.

Men began to fall in a higher volume all of a sudden, as the invisible guns, obscured by the rolling cloud of smoke and dust, began to blindly fire in front of them, hoping to hit one of the oncoming silhouettes.

I wanted to be able to switch my hearing off for a moment, the never-ending pounding from the artillery a blaring backdrop to the noise of raking gunfire, and awful screeches of dying men. The uproar was orchestral, each sound wishing to compliment the other in the most grotesque way possible, the assault on my eardrums never letting up for a second.

For a moment, it felt as though my very brain was being tormented, shaken around violently by the pandemonium and the tremoring earthquake that rattled away at the ground that I stood on.

Somehow, my feet continued to pull me forwards, not wanting me to be left behind and thought of as a coward. I had managed to catch up with the rest of the platoon, just as I saw Roger Nash let three bullets pass straight through his body, as if he was a thin sheet of paper. The bullets carried on as if they had struck nothing, as Nash simply sunk to his knees, falling face down into the mud, splattering muck and blood all over his personal territory.

I watched as the Germans advertised their whereabouts, tiny flickers of lights as round after round was thrown our way, the distinctive *rat-tat-tat* of a machine gun firing somewhere over to my left.

The machine gun seemed to be aiming low, as I watched men suddenly drop to the ground, clutching away at their shin bones, now fully exposed thanks to the small round that had ripped away at their flesh.

Bullets began thwacking into the ground on my right, smaller explosions of dirt than the artillery that I had come to expect, signifying to me the arrival of bullets. The line of mini explosions continued, charging its way towards me, making me instinctively drop to the ground with a splash, coating myself head to toe in a makeup of mud and blood.

The bullets continued raking their way towards me, as I begin to crawl to the nearest shell hole that I could get to, without turning back. Using my rifle as a gripping stick, I dug it into the loose ground and dragged myself along, falling headfirst into another pool of water at the bottom.

I bounced off something as I closed my eyes and braced for the cold water to submerge me and, as I opened my eyes, I recognised the bloke from the same company as me, although I could not remember his name.

Half of his neck seemed to be missing, as he sat, almost upright at the bottom of the hole, to the point where it could be mistaken that he was taking a nap in amongst all the chaos.

His eyes had already glazed over and had started to sink back into his skull, which is how I left him, scrabbling my way to the top, not wanting to be anywhere near anything that might bring me some bad luck.

I froze at the top of the shell hole, as I realised that I was about to vomit. I wanted to carry on moving forward, to be with the rest of the men, but something was stopping me from doing so.

The clumpy mud continued to be thrown in all directions by the artillery that still threatened to rip me into pieces, as the machine guns continued to rain horizontal terror upon us; men's chests being ripped open and skulls being shattered.

"Why have you stopped!" screamed a voice from just behind me, sounding as if he was straining so much that his throat was red-raw.

"Keep moving! That way!" he bellowed, as he took a hold of my webbing and tugged me forwards, before he himself stopped.

His head lolled from side to side for a moment, as if he had lost the ability to hold his head upright and was struggling to stay awake.

As I looked over at him, I realised that it was Corporal

Milne, one of the platoon section NCOs, who had found me rooted to the spot, refusing to go on.

I could make out his short, sharp breaths even above the din, as if he wanted deeper, longer breaths but was interrupted by some sort of obstruction in his windpipe.

As he dropped to the ground, I saw that he did; a twisted, jagged piece of shell sticking almost proudly from the side of his neck. He fell to his knees at first, and as I tried to grab him, to stop him from falling face down into the dirt, I realised that there was an equally large chunk of shrapnel embedded in his lower chest, right where I estimated his lungs would be.

I released my rifle, letting it fall to the ground with a splash, as I gently laid the corporal out on his back, leaving him to die in a slightly more comfortable position than if he was to drown himself in amongst the mud.

My breath began to fail, and my feet still refused to work. I didn't want to run towards that cloud of smoke, where the fires were raging, and bullets were flying. It was my natural instinct to jump into the bottom of a shell hole, clutch my rifle and curl up into a ball. I wanted this all to be over.

I knew, even in my confused and helpless state, that if I was to do that, I would end up dead anyway, the victim of a firing squad at dawn the next morning. I had to keep moving.

I began to search for someone I knew, a figure that I could follow and possibly hide behind, but I could see no one.

I forced myself to begin charging forwards, in the hope that I would see someone that I vaguely recognised, and give me some sort of assurance.

Suddenly, I caught a flash of some stripes. I fixed my eyes upon him, and lifted my heavy, sticky boots high up into my chest, running over towards him.

As I got closer, I could just about hear his voice, as he guided everyone in.

"Etwell, get up to that cart there. Hawling cover his run!"

The sucking glooping noise that I made as I ran over to him, as he perched behind half an old stone wall, must have been louder than the crescendo of flying bullets and artillery shells, as he turned to witness the pathetic, lanky private stumble his way towards him.

"Ellis! Over here! Into me, now!"

I wasn't going to take any chances, Sergeant Needs was one of the most experienced soldiers in the whole of the army, he was like a father to me. I was going to do exactly what he told me to do.

2

"Lads, that crater there. That's where we're going. See it?"

The sergeant was calm. His short, to the point instructions were met with agreements from the few men that he now had under his command.

"Ferguson, Shaw, Mackie. Give us some cover while we make it over. Then come to us. Got it?"

There were a few more mutters of agreement, that would have been like shouts had it not been for the pounding of shells and machine guns that were incessant in their delivery of death.

"Ready? Then let's go."

The three men poked their heads bravely over the top of the wall, as they fired a volley of bullets back in the direction of the Germans, probably the first taste of incoming rifle fire that they had had all morning.

As soon as the first round kicked out of their weapons, Sergeant Needs was already on his feet, screaming.

"Follow me! Let's go! Move!"

We all did as we were told, following quite literally in his footsteps, convinced that the experience and knowledge of the battlefield that he possessed, would somehow protect him and us in our advance.

The man in front of me suddenly spun round, as a round caught him in the top of his shoulder, sending him crashing to the ground, just missing me by inches.

"Leave him! Don't stop!" came the voice from behind me, as we mercilessly left the man to scream out for his mother in a concoction of sodden earth and his own blood.

I closed my eyes for a moment, forcing myself to forget about him in a cold, clinical manner. It was against my nature, but these men had all been over the top before, they knew what to do to give themselves a small chance at survival, and I intended to try my hardest to make it through.

Bullets fizzed and cracked into the ground all around me, some whispering into my ear as they flew past, as they desperately tried to cut down the group of men that had suddenly emerged from the flames and smoke.

I watched as the Sergeant seemed to leap high into the air, as if he was trying to vault the entire crater, before he came smashing down on the far side of it, expertly avoiding the pit of water that the rest of us all splashed into.

"Jam tins! Jam tins! Who's got them!" I was in awe of Needs as he continued to take complete control of the situation, managing to face up to the reality that he could be dead in a few moments, apparently putting it to the back of his mind.

A few of the men in the hole began shuffling around,

before they produced small, circular tins, the kind that we got our milk rations in, now stuffed with anything that they could find that would somehow cause a nuisance to the enemy. Protruding from the top of the lid was a small wick, ready to be lit and thrown.

The sergeant, perched on the edge of the shell hole, surveying the scene before him, began to fumble around, pulling himself a cigarette from his packet and shoving it into his mouth.

"On my say so, lob them into the trench. Harris, Dalton, Nash; you're the first into the dugout. Then the rest follow on."

He spoke with such a conviction that not one man wanted to offer up any sort of protestation at being the first men into the enemy trench, essentially being used as bait to determine how many enemy troops were still alive.

"Beattie, light them up. Might as well light me while you're at it."

"Sarge," replied Beattie, as he began to rummage around under his shirt to pull out the packet of matches that he kept in his underpants, to keep them dry.

Beattie lit the sergeant's cigarette first, before using the last few seconds of his match to light the first jam tin, Sergeant Needs lighting the other two with the tip of his ciggy.

The fuses fizzed away nicely, the men clutching hold of them nervously looking over at the sergeant, awaiting his go signal, as he continued to defiantly stare out over the top of the hole. His cigarette bobbed around in his mouth as he persisted in puffing away on it, before spitting it out on the ground next to him.

"Now! Go! Throw them!"

The three men threw the tins, as if they were one body, towards the trench, the aggressive hissing passing away to the point where we could no longer hear them.

"You three, now!" he screamed, not even looking back to direct them, just a swift flick of the arm told them that their curtain was rising.

Just as the three of them emerged from the hole, there was an ear popping bang, one far louder than an artillery shell could ever have been, as the enemy trench was engulfed in a huge cloud of nails and metal fragments.

I inched my way up to the top of the hole, to take a look at what was going on, just as I watched the three figures leap their way into the German trench, ready to take on whoever and whatever lay in wait for them. I marvelled at their bravery as I watched the last head disappear below the parapet. It was a courage that I wished I possessed, and hoped to gain, as I rubbed shoulders with these heroes. According to Private Sargent, the only other soldier in the platoon who had joined up after the war's outbreak, bravery came with experience, which was something that I was distinctly lacking in. I had only been in France for two weeks.

"Whenever you're ready, Ellis!" Sergeant Needs screamed as he stood confidently atop the shell hole, the others already having vacated and charged towards the trench. Feeling like I was letting the side down, I hopped up, ready to follow suit.

I snagged my trousers on a coil of barbed wire, destroyed so expertly by the artillery bombardment that had ended not five minutes before. It ripped at my trousers and bit away at the surface of my lower leg, threatening to entangle me in its snares. Gripping it tightly, ignoring the pain that was sent sparking through my hand, I ripped it away forcefully, feeling the small flecks of blood fly around as I did so.

I caught up with Sergeant Needs just as he was sliding his way into the trench and I watched as his head bobbed below the parapet, before I was coated in another fresh helping of dirt and dust.

Thankful to be getting out of the open ground and away from the constant shellfire and machine guns, I hopped down into the trench, hitting the fire step half a second later.

The trench was deep, far deeper than our own, probably dug at a depth of at least six feet, with another foot or two of sandbags around the top. The parados at the back of the trench was probably more than a foot taller than at the front, presumably to help protect the poor souls who occupied this part of the line.

By my calculations there were seven of us standing in that trench, which had meant that we had lost three others on our way from the shell hole to the German stronghold. It was a fact that not one of us acknowledged as we stood there.

The section of trench that we hid in seemed relatively quiet, compared to the onslaught of death and destruction that lay just outside of here. But, we all knew that as soon as the Germans had word that their front line was gone, the shells would soon be redirected to fall right onto our heads.

Sergeant Needs took control of the situation once again, choosing to point at individuals and move his hands around in such a way that he gave us silent instructions.

Beattie, Harris, Dalton and Nash were to move off to the left, while Sergeant Needs, Etwell and I would move off to the right of the trench, hopefully clearing a decent enough section that meant we met up with the rest of the advance.

Instantly, everyone swung into action, moving slowly and deliberately in the quiet, the earlier smashing of artillery now just a faint rumbling in my ears. The trench was built in a zig zag formation, and I looked behind me, just to catch the sight of Beattie disappearing around the far side of the section.

We soon followed suit, Etwell at the front of our small column, Sergeant Needs bringing up the rear, with me, the inexperienced young private in the middle.

Our rifles, especially with the sharpened point of the bayonet fixed to it, seemed cumbersome in the confined nature of the trenches, making it difficult to swing round corners and bring them up to aim.

The trench was damp, but not sodden, the wooden boards on the floor were raised above the ground level of the trench ever so slightly, so that the Germans' feet didn't get wet, something that I was very grateful for at that moment in time. The parapet was high and well protected with sandbags, the sides consolidated well with a mixture of corrugated iron and branches to offer a sturdier structure.

The fire step that ran along the length of the trench was littered with everything that might be needed for a night on the frontline; playing cards, cigarettes and even a mouth organ was perched there. Open cans of food lay on their side, obviously abandoned by the retreating troops, gratefully to be accepted by the rats that were gradually making their way out of their own bunkers.

Our footsteps thumped forebodingly on the wooden boards as we approached the end of our first section of trench.

As we got to the end, Etwell stopped, lowered his rifle and pressed his back into what was now the front of the trench. He looked across at the two figures behind him, ensuring that they were ready to manoeuvre around the corner. I suddenly noticed that he had lost his cap.

He nodded to us both, before bringing his rifle back up and edging around the corner of the trench, swinging his rifle up accusingly as he did so.

Suddenly, there was a whacking noise, the kind that is made when a number one batman smashes a full toss all the way out to the boundary. The smacking noise was accompanied by a low growl from Etwell, reciprocated by an even louder bellow from another figure, clearly not scared in the slightest who he might wake up as he screamed.

The sergeant and I stood rooted to the spot for half a second, which was just enough time to watch Etwell and an accompanying German soldier cannon into the back of the trench, as I watched the wind explode from his lungs in doing so.

The German had hit Etwell's rifle with his own, and was now proceeding to press it as hard as he could into Herbert's throat, to suffocate the life out of him.

Etwell was a broad shouldered, muscular man, powerful enough to rugby tackle a horse to the ground if he needed to, but he was struggling against this man, on account of the fact that he was having his windpipe slowly crushed.

Etwell kicked out into the German's groin, but still he refused to budge his clamp on Etwell's neck, forcing it into the back of the trench as much as he could.

I felt like I should do something, maybe run my bayonet through the German, saving Etwell, but I was too scared to face what was around the corner of the trench.

What if one of his friends was camped there waiting for me?

"Shoot him! Ellis, shoot him!" Etwell croaked, as he began to rasp for air, his face turning a vehement red, legs bucking and kicking in frustration.

A gunshot suddenly exploded right behind my head, rendering me completely deaf, as the sergeant squeezed his way next to me, leaning up against the back of the trench to take the shot at the offending German.

As if the man had simply been switched off, he slumped into the wall of the trench, as Etwell dropped his rifle and fell to his knees, gasping for air.

Sergeant Needs stepped forward and mercilessly put his bayonet through the German's chest, stopping the sucking, gurgling noises that were pitifully muttering from the back of his throat. He said nothing to me as he strode past.

"Why didn't you shoot him?" Etwell said, trying to shout but succeeding in only rasping and spitting at me, "Did you want me to die?"

"I-I'm…sorry," I stuttered.

"Sorry? You do that again and I'll run you through myself. Pull yourself together."

I felt humiliated by the short episode and wanted

nothing more than to have the whole offensive over and done with, so that I could focus on simply getting through the next day. Every day was one day closer to getting back home safely, I told myself.

"We'll have to move quickly now," Sergeant Needs piped up, "the gunshot will have told them we're here. Etwell, you're in the middle, deep breaths."

Etwell pushed me to the back of our trio, still clutching and massaging his neck, as Sergeant Needs took the front.

As one body, we began to inch our way down the next section of the trench, passing an abandoned sharpshooter's point that was heavily sandbagged and well camouflaged.

I walked backwards, covering our rear slowly, Etwell checking every couple of paces that I was still with them. Suddenly, a woollen blanket, pulled over a small recess in the trench was thrown backwards, a young German soldier leaping out of it, as if he had slept through the artillery bombardment and subsequent offensive.

Instinctively, I swung my rifle round, slashing him straight across his stomach as he moved towards me. At first, it seemed like I hadn't made more than a superficial cut to his skin but after half a second more, he winced as the excitement in his body began to subside and the pain took hold.

Come on. Stick it in him. Finish him off. He's the enemy.

He stared at me with innocent, unbelieving eyes for a moment, as if he was disappointed in me somehow.

"I'm sorry," I whispered gently to him, as he dropped his rifle and clutched at his stomach, in agony.

"Finish him!" growled Etwell in my ear, "Now, do it!"

I stared at the blood which was now resident on the end of my bayonet, not able to take in the damage that I had done to this young boy and his family. Someone, somewhere, was going to miss him, he would become an empty place at the dinner table, just like any of the other British soldiers who had been cut down today.

"What's the matter with you!" Etwell rasped, as he plunged his bayonet into the young German's chest silently, twisting it around in his body for a moment, before withdrawing coolly. "You are weak, Ellis. You better start showing something soon. You're a liability."

He was right, although he expressed it with so much malice in his voice that I wanted to take a bullet to the skull.

"Alright, Etwell. It's his first time. Let's focus."

We stood in silence for a moment or two, as the rattle of machine guns somewhere in the distance, coupled with the ever-present artillery, continued to boom under foot. Then, pushing himself from the wall of the trench, Sergeant Needs got back to work.

"Okay let's go."

Exhaling sharply, Needs rounded the corner to the trench, instinctively raising his rifle into his shoulder, stopping just short of pulling his trigger.

"Cor, that was a close one mate," he said, lowering his weapon until it was no longer a threat. "Friends," he sighed, looking over to us, as he took a step back to let the other soldiers see us.

"Naik Singh, Sergeant," he declared, proudly, shouldering his weapon casually. "Second Battalion, Garhwalis."

"You were on our right flank."

"And you on our left, Sergeant," he said with a slight smile.

"So, that means we're clear."

"Yes. I believe so."

Sergeant Needs shook his head for a moment, taking in the most recent revelation and working out what to do next.

"How many men have you got with you, Singh?"

"Fifteen or sixteen, Sergeant."

"Stretch them out along these three sections of the trench. I'll spread mine out over the next few. Understood?"

"Yes, Sergeant."

He disappeared around the corner, before I could hear him chattering away to his men on his side of the wall.

"Right then, we'll move back this way, link up with the others and wait for orders."

I began to feel hungry as I realised that, for now, the action was over and that I had made it. I had survived the treacherous journey across No Man's Land and made it into the Germans' trenches. All without having fired a single shot from my rifle.

Although I felt good, I realised that I had messed up. I hadn't exactly been expecting to become a regimental war hero, but I had failed to have even killed the enemy when they threatened one of my fellow platoon members.

If I knew anything about Etwell, I was in for a right rollicking just as soon as we had recovered.

3

Physically and emotionally, I had come a long way since I had arrived in France, and it hadn't seemed all that long ago that Corporal Milne had been introducing me to the rest of the platoon.

"Welcome, Ellis," he said with an outstretched arm and a slight, mocking bow, "to Chesney Wold."

I looked at him with a smirk on my face and an inquisitive eye, "Chesney Wold?"

"Yes, Chesney Wold, Ellis. That's what I said," he rolled his eyes towards the other members of the platoon, "are you all completely uneducated? Has *no one* ever read Dickens?"

"I told you, Milne. No one reads that sort of book anymore, only the old people like you read them still. Corporal Beattie," the man said, pulling his cigarette from his mouth as he did so.

"*Acting* Corporal Beattie, Sam," Milne said, as if he had said it a thousand times before.

"Yeah, well, it's only a matter of time before he bites it

and I'll be the corporal around 'ere," he said with a wink. "The girls don't know the difference anyway."

"Chesney Wold was the estate from Bleak House, Ellis. It isn't exactly chirpy here, hence Chesney Wold," he proclaimed proudly, as if he enjoyed educating people that didn't know quite as much as he did.

"Anyway, that's Beattie. Over there is our sergeant, who is also a private, he joined up after the war started, like you. The rest of us are professionals."

"Meant to be," the figure remarked, offering out a hand for me to take. "Private Robert Sargent. Their idea of a joke," he said, rolling his eyes at the sniggering corporal and the rest of his men.

"Yeah, meant to be," Milne continued, "that's Harris, and over there...is Etwell." The figure barely even looked up to acknowledge he was being spoken to, but instead continued to wipe down his bayonet, inspecting the state of his face from the gleam that it gave off. "Yoo-hoo, Etwell. Are you coming out to play today?"

"Go home, Milne," he said, still avoiding having to lift his head up to join the conversation.

"Etwell," Milne continued, under his breath, "is our platoon nutcase. Every platoon has one. Etwell is ours."

I stayed quiet, not wanting to subject myself to a tirade of abuse that I expected from a man as rough looking as Etwell. Even though he was sitting down, he had a commanding presence, square jawed and broad, he was built like a Greek god. He frowned defiantly into his bayonet, and for some reason I got the sense that he was growing furious with his own reflection, not wanting to back down.

"His girl left him for someone else a few weeks ago,

only just heard. He's a little bit angry. Blames the Germans. He is on our side, promise."

I gave the corporal a slight smirk in return, as he looked around the trenches to find something else to tell me about.

"This is our trench anyway. The Germans, are in that direction. Don't bother looking for them as they'll find you before you see them. If you know what I mean."

"Sharpshooters," Sargent piped up, "he likes to talk in riddles. You get used to it."

I looked back at the corporal, a broad grin right the way across his face. "Some do, some don't lad. Anyway, make yourself at home."

It hadn't taken me too long to fit into the monotony of the daily routine of the frontline; early morning stand-to, followed by breakfast, then hours of milling about and sleeping, just waiting for the evening stand-to. I was grateful to be rotated off the frontline after four days. But we were soon back again, gearing up for an offensive.

I never had got quite used to the way that Milne had liked to talk, and now, I never would, as he was lying out in No Man's Land, waiting for the rats and maggots to begin eating away at his flesh. I bet he was still grinning though.

He wasn't the only member of the platoon that was no longer with us. I hadn't seen the likes of Hawling, Nash or Shaw for well three hours now, and the chances were I never would again, not alive anyway.

I supposed that they had all met a similar fate to Corporal Milne, lying face down in the dirt somewhere, silently accepting of the fact that they were no longer on this mortal realm.

Slaughter Fields

I felt guilty in some ways, that the men that had gone down today had been the professional soldiers, the ones who had been dispatched out here as soon as war was declared. They had been through rigorous and thorough training, and most had seen some sort of deployment in one of the far corners of the Empire, only to have been cut down by bullets and bombs just a couple of hundred miles away from Britain.

Sargent and I had signed up after the war had been declared, and had merely been two additions to the company after they had arrived in France. Bob had got to the front before I had, but was mightily glad that I had arrived when I did, so that I could take over the baton of platoon scapegoat.

Out of the platoon strength of almost fifty men, we had just enough remaining to scrape together one section of twelve. I could only hope that all the other companies involved had fared far better than we had done. We had been completely decimated.

I took another sip of water, clamping my mouth shut immediately after and holding my hand up, to stop the urge to vomit it all straight back up again and waste what could be my last bit of water for hours.

I had already thrown up on three separate occasions in the twenty minutes or so after the advance, the images of bodies sitting sodden at the bottom of shell holes and men with no limbs hopping around out in No Man's Land, running rampant in my mind.

Fortunately, I hadn't been the only one to have done so, Sargent and Beattie spewing up watery substances along the sides of the trenches also, much to the disgust of men like Etwell.

"Pathetic," he had muttered as I coughed up the yellowy remnants of my stomach lining, "you'll never make a real soldier."

I didn't have time to retaliate, even if I had wanted to, as several officers began to charge down the trenches, issuing orders to any men that they could find.

"Start shoring up those parapets gentlemen, prepare for a counter-attack."

Sergeant Needs began to issue specific orders to us, making sure that we wouldn't fall foul of the senior officer's typically vague commands.

"You two, go and find some sacks, the engineers should have them. Then start stuffing them. Beattie, Ellis, start clearing up that rubble there, pack it back into the wall. I don't want that collapsing."

He continued to issue order after order, even choosing to ignore the muttering of Etwell, protesting about wanting to at least have a little break before being thrust back into work. I admired the way that Needs was working, coolly and professionally, making sure that everyone pulled their weight, including him.

Ever since I had met him I was struck by his stature and how he seemed to have a hold over his men. I couldn't quite work out what it was. Admiration? Maybe. Fear? Possibly. Whatever it was, it worked in this platoon, and he wasn't going to let that slip just because we'd had less than an hour's worth of fighting.

I was horrified, as Beattie and I began to dig out the collapsed section of trench, to discover two bodies buried under the mound, both young Germans, one with no legs attached. I felt like being sick again, but I didn't have the energy nor the substance for anything to come out, I just stood and stared at them for a moment, their waxy skin already losing their natural colour.

"What's the matter, Ellis?" the sergeant queried.

"The bodies, Sergeant Needs. Wh-what do we do with them?" I thought I could make out a few chuckles and sniggers from the other lads, which were soon hushed up as the sergeant spoke.

"We leave them, Ellis. Move them out of the way if you want, but don't waste your time on them. Defence is our priority. That's what will keep you alive, son."

I jumped as I began tugging at one of the bodies, submerged by the rubble, as I heard a low groan, which turned into a shout. Beattie began to laugh.

"Relax, Ellis. It's not him. It's coming from out there. This always happens."

I stood, for a moment, trying to make sense of what he meant, as the groans turned into yells, and I realised they weren't coming from the trench, but from No Man's Land.

"When the artillery stops, you can always hear them. Plus, those that have been knocked out wake up, right about now. You'll get used to it."

I didn't see how I could, the screams were horrifying, as I was forced to listen to the tormented souls for hours afterwards, while we tried our best to make this trench our own.

"The artillery will keep them quiet in a bit, don't worry."

"Our artillery?"

"We'd be lucky. No, the Germans. They'll be a bit miffed that we've got their trench now, to tell you the truth. Surprised it hasn't come down yet."

I was beginning to feel even more helpless now than when I had done when I was back in Britain. There seemed like there would be no end to the rainfall of shells and the monotony of a machine gunner's bullets until we were safely back behind the line, which was going to be a number of days away at the very least.

"You got a girlfriend then, Ellis?" Beattie suddenly piped up, clearly cottoning onto the fact that I wasn't exactly feeling optimistic at that moment in time.

"No," I retorted defensively, taking even myself by surprise.

"Alright, alright, I was only asking. Don't bite my 'ead off."

"Sorry," I conceded, "I'm just feeling a little jumpy. What about you?"

"Eh?"

"A girl, you got one back at home?"

"Back at home?" called Harris from the other side of the trench, now enjoying a cigarette. "He's got about four in the village not five miles from here! And that's not counting the one that he met when we first arrived in France!"

I waited for Beattie to refute the claims, but all that met my gaze was a wry smile, and a slight shrug.

"I could be dead tomorrow," he muttered, quite without a care. It surprised me somewhat, as he was an unremarkable fellow; he was of quite a slight build and medium in height, coming up a few inches shorter than I was. His eyes were bland, which seemed to match his hair and, in amongst all the dirt that he had acquired over his skin and uniform, he was completely ordinary.

"He is, Ellis, known as a Poodle faker."

Slaughter Fields

"Now that is too far," Beattie suddenly sparked up, jabbing a finger towards Harris, who was now laughing so hard that I thought he might suck us all into the giant vortex that was his mouth.

"I am *not* a Poodle faker," Beattie said, trying earnestly to defend himself, "I just like talking to women is all."

I hadn't heard of the phrase Poodle faker when I arrived on the frontline, but ever since, it was one that I heard on more than one occasion to describe the gentleman whose pursuits seemed to lead them into a woman's bedroom, just as often as a loyal poodle did.

"The sprog doesn't believe you, Sam! Look at his face!" I enjoyed being accepted into their circles of mickey taking and gentle prodding, but I wasn't sure on the nickname that they had selected for me; 'the sprog.' I did not know what to make of it either, whether it was a term of brotherly affection, or merely an attempt to bait me, something which I was not quick in taking.

"Yeah well, just because you lot seem to want to be killed, doesn't mean I have to stop talking to the lovely ladies around here. Who knows, I could be leaving France with a lovely Mrs Beattie on my arm."

"Paa haa, you'll be lucky!"

"Yeah well, either way, I'm still better with the ladies than you Dougie," Beattie said directed towards Harris, as he stopped what he was doing to withdraw a cigarette from his top pocket. He shoved the packet under my nose, giving a gentle nod to take one. I shook my head.

"Still? Blimey. You're going to have to start eventually mate."

"I give it three more days," piped up Sargent, "once he really starts getting stuck in he'll realise he needs them."

I wondered what he had meant by that, especially as he had only been in France for four weeks longer than I had. But then again, I reasoned, I had only been here two weeks and I hadn't seen a single German in all that time and now, here I was, preparing to sleep in their trenches.

And I still hadn't fired a single round from my rifle.

4

I felt my legs twitching as someone began to kick me awake, gently at first, before growing impatient at my apparent reluctance to wake up from my slumber.

Sleeping on the fire step hadn't been all that uncomfortable, but I couldn't quite believe that it was already my turn on watch, after what had felt like less than five minutes of sleep.

A small gas lantern hissed away in the corner of the trench, and I could just about make out the flickering faces of Beattie and Sargent as they played a quick game of cards with one another. Etwell was perched on the makeshift fire step, the one that had hastily been set up facing what was now our frontline.

I could make out the broad, wide shouldered outline of Sergeant Needs as he stood watching over me, like he had been my guardian angel for the whole time that I had been asleep. He turned his head towards the others, so that he caught his face in the light and I could make out almost every feature of his aging, rough face. He had some sort of crater next to his left eye, where a piece of shrapnel had embedded itself just above his cheek bone some months before.

"Ellis, come on," he half-whispered half-shouted at me, tapping me on the feet for a third time. Sensing some sort of urgency in his voice, I bolted upright, ready to face a German attack if there was one heading our way. The speed with which I got up, grabbed the others' attention.

"Right, listen in," declared Sergeant Needs, making Beattie drop his playing cards and reach for his cap. "We're moving further north, to reinforce the line there and shore up our left flank. We'll be heading into the German's reserve trenches, they've abandoned them completely. Reinforcements are headed here to allow for a better defence. Apparently, we are a depleted company at the moment."

"You don't say," Harris muttered under his breath.

"Grab your kit. We'll move in five minutes, how does that sound?"

We didn't have much to grab, most of it was either already left behind in the town five miles away, some French locals operating a sort of locker system for the fighting troops, or it was strapped firmly into the pouches of our webbing. We would be ready in about thirty seconds. Still, it was nice not to feel so rushed.

"Oh, and by the way," he said, almost as an afterthought, "seeing as the Lieutenant has put his wooden overcoat on, I'm now acting as the platoon commander. So, best behaviour."

"Always for you, Sergeant," Harris said mockingly, blowing a series of kisses over towards him, which the sergeant took in his stride.

"So then, Sergeant," Beattie said, hopping up from his stool to fall in behind Needs, "does this mean I'm a *full* corporal now?"

"No, Acting Corporal Beattie, it does not. Only an officer can deal with that kind of dizzying promotion."

The lads all began sniggering, as Beattie turned dejectedly away to go and grab his rifle.

"Don't know why you're all laughing," he said sulkily, "I'm still higher up the food chain than you lot."

"So, that's that then," Bob Sargent declared, "Lieutenant Fairweather is gone then."

"I always knew he'd get a goodnight kiss," Harris chimed in, "he had that sort of face…Shame though, I kind of liked him."

I had too, he had been kind to me from the first day that I had joined the platoon. He hadn't been overly friendly, but he had made himself accessible enough that I felt like I was able to take my various concerns to him, when they had cropped up.

Etwell had been the reason for the first visit that I had made to see Lieutenant Fairweather, the first time that he had threatened to shoot me for being far too young to be on the front line. I wasn't a sensitive soul, but it had affected me and I had seen no other option than to request a transfer to a different platoon, or at the very least to a different section, so that I didn't have to spend as much of my day with the awful bloke.

"The thing about Etwell is," Lieutenant Fairweather had said with a sigh, "he's trapped in his own little world. It's all so black and white to him, but he can't seem to let anyone else in. He is convinced that everyone here is going to die, so he doesn't want to get close to anyone. It's done out of an affection really."

I had tried to protest somewhat with him, but the Lieutenant was adamant, "He is a damn fine soldier, Ellis. A brilliant one. He'd make a fantastic NCO if it wasn't for his temper. Just stay on the right side of him and you'll be fine, he knows that he's not allowed to be a fighter anymore."

I wasn't exactly comforted by Lieutenant Fairweather's words, but he had the discretion to mention it to no one, which I was grateful for. He may have made no further mention on the subject, but I was acutely aware that he was keeping half an eye on the situation, and I was convinced that Etwell knew it too.

"Fairweather wasn't the only one to cop it," chimed in Bob Sargent, as we descended into a melancholic recital of all the men from the platoon that we had seen gunned down, earlier on in the day. "Hawling went down like a sack of spuds. Oh, and Saunders went out for a duck as well."

"That was his first time out? I didn't know that. Oh, now that is a shame, I liked him."

Harris continued with the grotesque roll call, "Then there's Nash, Shaw and Harrison. Actually, did anyone see Harrison go down?" No one answered, but all just sat in an empty silence, before he answered his own question, "'Cos I didn't."

"Apparently," Beattie added, trying to move the tone along from all the men that we knew that were now dead, "the Garhwalis got hit pretty bad today."

"Oh right, did they?" Etwell growled in a rare occasion of joining in with a conversation. "That's funny because

Slaughter Fields

so did we." He marched over to Beattie to look him dead in the eyes.

"Yeah...I know that. C'mon Herb, we're just trying to make conversation."

Etwell spun away from him, making to grab his kit, as I caught Beattie raising his eyebrows to Harris. Suddenly, Etwell spun around again, facing all of us.

"You missed someone off the list. I bet you don't even know who it is," he only gave us half a second to think before he began to launch into his next phase of speech. "Corporal Milne. Remember him?"

I did. I knew we all did. But no one said anything, for fear that Etwell would suddenly turn on one of us and smash seven bells out of us. I could just about make out Beattie making his way slowly towards Etwell's rifle, doing us all a favour.

"Corporal Daniel Milne," he repeated, which sent a shockwave of guilt and embarrassment surging around my body and I immediately felt like Etwell was directing his ramblings towards me.

Milne had been the one who had stopped for me during the advance, only for a second or two, but that was all that it had taken. If I hadn't frozen to the spot during that advance, then he wouldn't have had to have paused to grab me. If only he hadn't stopped, he could have been a few yards further ahead than what he was, which meant that the twisted shrapnel wouldn't be hanging arrogantly from his neck, nor would a similar piece be protruding from his chest.

It had all been my fault. In that moment I realised that I owed my life to Milne, on more than one count. If I had stayed frozen where I was, I would have been cut down by German bullets, a perfect stationary target that anyone could have used as practice. But also, because, if he hadn't been standing where he was, those shell fragments would have ripped their way through my skin, and not his. I should have been dead, and I knew that Etwell could tell I had come to that realisation, from the look on my face.

"It was you! If you hadn't stopped, he would still be alive! We were going to make it through this war, together. Now, I have nothing, absolutely nothing in my life that is worth living for."

He took two paces towards me and came so close into my face that he spat over me as he spoke, his warm breath intertwining with mine as he stood there.

"You better buck your ideas up. A good soldier died for you. A good man. All you're good for is making us look over our shoulders to check you're coming with us."

"Oi, come on now Etwell, that's enough. It's not all down to him. You've had your release," I felt Bob sidle up next to me.

"No, you're right," he said, stepping away from me slightly, as if he was conceding, "It's not all down to him. It's you too. You helped to kill Milne."

"Eh? How'd you figure that one out?"

"You shouldn't even be 'ere. You're the kind of blokes that are going to get us all killed. You should have stayed at home! You should have left it to us professionals. It took the Germans *years* to build up their army, years and years of hard graft and training. And what have we got? Four hundred thousand teenagers in six weeks they're telling us. Four hundred thousand spotty, *weak* teenagers who suddenly decide they want to help! What chance do we stand?!"

Accusingly, he stepped back up in to both of our faces, "You should have just let us professionals deal with it, not help us to a quick death."

I opened my mouth to defend myself, but instantly knew that I had made the wrong decision as Etwell bolted for me.

"Got something to say have you, Sprog?"

I was grateful that Beattie was closer to Etwell's rifle than he was, as I was sure that if it had been within his grasp he would be burying round after round in my gut.

"That's enough Etwell," Sergeant Needs eventually said, trying to shove a massive shoulder in between Etwell's face and mine. "Go over there and take five, *now.*"

Sergeant Needs spoke forcefully, and with such a conviction that I felt like I was getting a dressing down in the process.

"He needs to learn how to fight, Sarge!" Etwell protested, his ears still steaming as he struggled to calm down over the loss of his friend.

"Yes, I agree," announced the sergeant, "he *will* get his chance, Etwell. Soon enough. You know that."

Sergeant Needs and Etwell continued to stare one another down, before the sergeant eventually came out on top, as Etwell backed away to gather up his things.

I was suddenly awash with feelings of inadequacy and incompetence, and for a moment I thought that Etwell was right.

I had failed miserably in what had been my first piece of action. I had rooted myself to the top of a shell hole and had practically waited for another man to die, before I found myself motivated to do anything.

I wasn't able to fire one single round to kill the murderous German that was clamping away at Etwell's neck. And I had found it even more impossible to finish off the young German who had caught himself on the end of my bayonet. I was a totally ineffective soldier.

I wondered how much longer it was possible for me to last, and considered simply walking out of the trench there and then, so that I was no longer a burden upon the rest of my platoon.

In the short space of twenty-four hours, I had gone from local hero, the young lad who had volunteered to go to war, to downright coward. I just couldn't understand why no one seemed to get the way that I was feeling.

It felt as if my brain had received a jolly good shaking, and all my thoughts were upside down and disorganised. I couldn't imagine that anyone else in this platoon had ever had the same feelings that I was currently experiencing, and for a moment, I didn't think that anyone had ever had the doubts and uncertainties over their capabilities that I was having, after Etwell's outburst.

As if he had been waiting around the corner, hiding until the sergeant had managed to diffuse the situation, a major, who I did not recognise, came marching around the corner.

"Where is Lieutenant Fairweather, I was told this was his platoon."

"Erm, he's not here, Sir," said Sergeant Needs, in a tone that was desperately hoping the major might take the hint that the platoon before him were not in want of being reminded that their Lieutenant was dead.

"Well, where is he then?" exclaimed the major, as if we were just one big inconvenience to him and his endless banquets.

I noticed that his uniform was impeccably clean, and that the only speck of dirt that seemed to be on him, was around the bottom of his leather boots, which looked like they had never been worn outside before that night. I didn't envy the batman who would have to spend the rest of the evening scrubbing them up.

I almost felt sorry for the major, walking into the platoon that was so on edge that we could have been toppled over by a slight breeze.

Etwell was the one who took the initiative, suddenly bursting open a German crate and pulling out a pistol. He rummaged around with it for a few seconds, before lifting his arm out, deadly straight as if he was pointing out the invisible stars and fired the flare gun into the sky.

There was a slight pause, as the major looked around at each of us totally bewildered, which was met with equally confused glares as to what Etwell might do next. Suddenly, the flare burst on its way back down to earth, slowly lingering over the No Man's Land that we had advanced across earlier.

A brilliant white light suddenly burst forth from the flare and Etwell had around eight to ten seconds to make his point to the major, before we were all plunged into the familiar darkness once again.

"He's up there, major," he said, stepping up on to the fire step for a moment, to look out over No Man's Land. "You see that broken cart over there? I think Lieutenant Fairweather is the third body to the right. I'm not one hundred per cent sure though."

We stood there for a moment, in total disbelief as to what he had just done, and I was sure that I wasn't the only one who was convinced that he had just guaranteed himself a meeting with a firing squad in the morning.

For the second time in the space of five minutes, it was down to Sergeant Needs to calm him down.

"Alright, Etwell," he said, beckoning him down from the fire step, just as the flare went out. "You've made your point. Sorry sir," he said, turning to the major, humbly. "It's been a long day for all of us. An emotional one too."

"Yes, well," the major almost scoffed, looking down his nose at the sergeant, "make sure you keep your men in check, sergeant. The next major he does that to might not be so kind."

"Of course, sir," mumbled Needs, offering up a half-hearted salute as the major turned away.

Beattie and Harris began sniggering in the corner of the section and, on the inside, I did too. None of us could quite believe that Etwell had actually got away with it.

"Right then you lot, come on. Let's go find our new bit of frontline, shall we?"

5

The tension within the platoon had seemed to have calmed down considerably immediately after Etwell's little outburst. Most of us simply went back to gathering up our things with a slight smile on our faces, hidden from the major as he skulked from the trench, quite pleased that Etwell had managed to have a go at one of the men who sent us into the fray.

We all found it rather amusing, that was, of course, apart from Etwell. He had his permanent scowl still etched across his face, as he lit up what must have been his fifth cigarette in as many minutes. He had always smoked heavily before, but as we settled in to our new line of defence, he was sucking in more drags of a ciggy, than he was oxygen.

The new section of trench was already vastly better than the one that we had been in previously. For starters, the walls hadn't succumbed to an artillery shell, which meant they were still high and sandbagged.

A new fire step had been added at several points along our frontline, with some sandbags removed to create little peep holes that you could poke your head through to have a quick look around. Sergeant Needs had also produced a periscope, which meant that we were even safer while we kept watch for a German counter attack.

Needs sat quietly in the corner of the trench, slightly separated from the rest of us, but still keeping a fatherly eye on what was his command. He had his notebook out, for the third time that day, and was furiously scribbling in it to while away the hours. I wondered what he could have been writing in there, whether it was his evaluation over how each of us had done today, a diary of some sorts or maybe even a letter to his wife.

He seemed to be a deeply thoughtful man, with no real beliefs or superstitions, but you could tell that he imagined every action in his mind before he did them. That was what must have made him an incredibly effective soldier.

All of a sudden, there was a solitary crack, and had it not been for the day's events, I would have simply thought that someone had just snapped a twig further down the line. But my now-accustomed mind didn't take too long to work out what it really was. A gunshot.

Nothing followed it apart from an eerie kind of silence, as everyone up and down the line, seemed completely fixed in their positions. No one moved a muscle, not even to grab their rifles or sit upright from their sleeping positions.

It felt like the whole of the western front had frozen to the spot.

Slaughter Fields

"What was that?" rasped Harris from somewhere in the darkness.

No one answered him for fear of what might happen to them if they spoke next. There was still a desperate void of noise, and I began to will someone, anyone to begin moving around so that we knew everything was okay.

Then we began to hear a rummaging sound, as clinking of kit and stumbling around began to take over.

Footsteps began to sound on the duckboards, at a steady leisurely pace, before cries of "Make way! Coming through!" erupted louder than an artillery shell ever could.

We all backed up onto the fire step, keeping the duckboards clear, as the first stretcher bearer slowly appeared from around the corner, splashing his way through the small puddle that had congregated there.

"Mind your backs!"

We all stared in a horrified silence as we watched the stretcher bearers manoeuvre their way around the trench, before I managed to get a good luck at the casualty who they were transporting.

He could not have been in my vision for much longer than three or four seconds, but what I laid my eyes upon, was just like it had been three or four hours.

The first thought that immediately passed through my mind was how lucky this young lad had been. I didn't know his name or even recognise him, but I knew he must have been from the regiment owing to the shoulder titles that bore the initials "RB" of the Rifle Brigade.

Somehow, the lad was still alive, and I wondered for a moment if he even knew what was going on with him right now, or if he could see me as his eyes fixed on to mine as he was stretchered past.

The boy that was carried past had managed to get himself shot, straight in his face. His whole face was a mangled piece of flesh, the parts of him that weren't, were instead drowning in his own blood. Even if I had known him, I doubt I would have been able to recognise him.

Just under his left eye, there was a large crater, about the size of a thrupenny bit, which was gushing blood faster than I could keep up with. I could make out the insides of his cheek, a vibrant pink in colour quite distinct and obvious from the scarlet crimson of his blood.

His cheek looked as though it had been torn apart, as easy as a damp piece of paper, and the skin began to flap and bob as he was tussled around on the canvas of the stretcher.

He didn't scream or make any kind of sound, but made the flow of blood infinitely worse as he tried to open and close his mouth, as if he was some sort of fish struggling to breathe when out of water.

"Keep still, lad. Come on, stay still," one of the stretcher bearers repeated, quite unsympathetically. I doubted that he was registering a single thing, but instead was in his own world of make-believe, where he was doing exactly what he wanted to do.

His eyes locked on to mine as he was dragged past, and, in that moment, I felt like I was watching my own corpse being taken away, after another miserable failing on my part, which had led to my own death.

I wondered if he would survive, or if the doctor's only

remedy would be to make him as comfortable as possible while he passed away. He had lost a lot of blood and before long, the pain would begin to set in, which would be excruciating.

As they disappeared around the corner of our trench, trying to find the temporary aid station that had been set up an hour or two before, Sergeant Needs began to shuffle around in his corner.

"Marksmen, lads. Be aware. *Always* be aware," he spoke with a sincerity that we all appreciated, like he actually cared enough to not want to see his men ending up in the same way.

The young lad stayed with me for hours afterwards, while everyone else found it easy to simply wipe the boy from their memory, and go back to what they had been doing beforehand.

As if he had sensed that I wouldn't have been able to erase the memory of the young soldier as quick as everyone else, Bob Sargent sidled up to me, offering me a cigarette.

"I give it one more day of this actually," he said as I declined his offer. "You can't keep on like this forever."

I wondered how long forever would actually last, as I was growing increasingly more defeatist in my outlook, especially as I had just seen someone carted out in front of me, gaping wound in the side of his face. I doubted that the young lad who had just copped one to the face had imagined that that was how he was about to end up, as if he did, he wouldn't have poked his head over the top.

"Forget about it, mate. It can happen to anyone. Just be thankful it wasn't you."

He paused as he leant his head down towards the match that was now hissing away at the end of his fingertips, before he flicked the stick away, letting it sizzle in the puddles underneath the wooden boards.

"So, why did you join up then?" he asked, chipperly.

I paused for a moment, to look at him. He flashed me a quick grin as he took the first initial puffs of smoke in, his green innocent eyes being shrouded in the mist caused by his exhalation of the smoke.

He was the same age as me, but I was confident that I had looked far more mature than he was and wondered if he had had to prove his age in any way when he had signed up. He was eighteen, but his face was so smooth and childlike, that he could have passed for anywhere around the fourteen mark. Coupled with his height, a good head and shoulders shorter than I was, and his skinny frame, it was possible to assume that this young soldier had only just left school to start working, never mind to go onto a battlefield.

"We've been through this before," I said, slightly irritable that he wasn't allowing me a few moments to wallow in the despair that I was currently harbouring at the bottom of my soul.

"I know," he chimed, "but it makes me feel good to know that there's someone else round here isn't a professional."

He stared at me expectantly, before I eventually rolled my eyes and gave in. "Alright, I was working in a bakery before here. My uncle's place. He took me in, trained me up, then left me to it. When it seemed like a war was coming I realised how boring my life was, so joined up two or three weeks before the declaration."

Slaughter Fields

He seemed happy that I had humoured him for a moment, before he began to chunter on about why he had joined up, without me even having to prompt him.

"My father wanted me to join up. He has his own tailor firm you see, but wanted me to have a bit of discipline and life experience before I took over. Now, it just looks like I'm going to die here," he scoffed, before falling into the pit of wallowing that I was already perched in.

Silently, he drew in drag after drag of his cigarette, before I decided it was my turn to drag him out of the hole.

"You have a girl?"

"Yeah," he said, watching the smoke from his own cigarette twist upwards into the night time air. "Used to think that I might marry her actually."

"You not going to now?"

"Nah," he said, trying desperately to hold back on his tears, "I'd much rather be killed here with you lot anyway."

He began to bounce his leg around nervously, as he tossed his cigarette up against the far side of the trench, almost angrily.

"Stupid war," he muttered, hauling himself to his feet. "Anyway," he sighed, slapping me on the shoulder, "don't take anything that these lot say to heart. I know what it's like to be where you are. They don't mean any of it."

"Anyone got any bumf?" Beattie declared, hopping down from the fire step and dancing around on his feet.

"Surely you don't need to go again, Sam," Harris sniggered.

"What? Thought I'd make the most of the German's

latrines while we're here. Before our luck turns and we end up back yonder."

"What luck?" sniggered Harris, before he pulled himself together to announce, "Think I saw some in that crate over there. I hope it stands up to the test."

"Cheers mate," he said slightly muffled, as he buried his head in the box, searching for the elusive toilet paper.

"How we looking with getting some extra rations, Sergeant?" queried Bob as Needs rounded the corner, staring into the pages of his trusty notebook.

"Not brilliant. But I'm hoping to get something in a little while, I'm due to see the Captain at zero three thirty. Hopefully I'll get something from him. How's everyone doing?"

"Good, Sergeant," came most of the replies, as we continually cleaned rifles, awaiting the next piece of action or excitement. I was just looking forward to making it through the night, when it was more likely that we would be allowed to get our heads down for some rest.

"Ellis? You okay?" he prompted.

"Y-yes, sarge. Good thanks," I lied. I knew that I wasn't going to be able to fool him, he was an experienced NCO, one that I was sure had dealt with the likes of me before. I respected him greatly, he was the one man that I had wanted to see when we had gone over the top, as I believed that he was the one that would be able to get me through this mess of a war.

"Good, good. Right then, there's no point in you all staying up on watch after the day we've had. Etwell and Harris, take the first watch with me. The rest of you, put your skulls down somewhere, you have two hours."

Not one of us needed to wait to be told again, within seconds, the gentle hums of exhausted soldiers snoring, was already wafting its way up and down the trench.

6
___

As I slowly began to come around, the darkness of the sky, still shrouded in the smoke from the shell blasts almost twenty-four hours ago now, made it more troublesome for me to find the energy to open my eye lids.

I could hear someone moving about close by, as if whoever it was wanted to sit exactly where I was propped up sleeping. I had my cloth hat pulled down over my face, to help me sleep, but also keep my exposed skin as warm as possible.

Eventually, I gave in, despite the groans of my body, that still screamed at me about how tired I really was, and I opened my eyes. Flicking my cap back onto the top of my head, I realised that it was Sergeant Needs who now perched at my feet, and I wondered how long he had been looking at me.

"Hello, Sarge."

"Good morning, Ellis."

He continued to stare at me, as if he was waiting for

me to start a conversation with him or do something that he had been expecting for a long while.

"Sorry Sarge, is it my turn on watch?"

He flicked his hand up in a way that told me not to worry, and as I caught sight of my wristwatch, I realised that it was four thirty in the morning. I still had half an hour to go before I was due up on the fire step. I could have had an extra bit of sleep.

Slightly annoyed with myself for waking up when I didn't need to, I began to shuffle around to get comfy again.

"Want some?" Sergeant Needs growled in my direction, offering a hip flask out to me.

"What is it?"

"Don't know. Some sort of French concoction, but it does the trick."

I decided to take his word for it, immediately regretting it, as I slid some of the paraffin tasting liquid down my throat. I coughed and rasped for a second or two, before going back for a second swig. It had grown on me more or less immediately.

"I'll put you in touch with the bloke who got it for me, if you like," he said, chuckling, "he can get his hands on almost anything. His name's Earnshaw. Funny little bloke really, but he offers a decent enough service."

I took a quick look at the flask, and noticed that it had a series of letters imprinted into the bottom of one side.

GRHMN.

He caught me staring at it with an inquisitive eye, deciding to answer my silent question before I got the opportunity to ask.

"My wife got it for me. George Robert and Helen Margaret Needs. She's sentimental like that, my wife." He paused for a moment as he clamped his giant hands back around it and looked at it himself for a moment, as if he had forgotten what it had inscribed upon it.

"She got it a few years ago for my thirtieth birthday. Married for nine years, and it was the first of my birthdays that we had managed to spend together, if you can believe it."

I could. I knew that he was a career soldier, and that he hadn't spent much of his time in Britain in recent years, instead being sent all over the empire to fight in various wars, put down sporadic uprisings and even ceremonial duties as and when the King had asked him to.

"Do you hate the Boche, Ellis?" His question took me by surprise, and I immediately found myself stuttering as I tried desperately to answer confidently and with conviction.

"Y-yes I do, Sergeant. Can't stand them." I wondered if this was some sort of a test of my character, to try and rile me up to hate the enemy even more than I already did, so that I might be able to fulfil my duties as an infantryman, rather than some sort of odd observer to the war.

He raised his eyebrows for a moment, before nodding his head ever so slightly. "Thought so, thought so. A lot of you do," he said, letting his speech hang tantalisingly in the air.

"I don't," he announced, quite proudly and without any hint of shame. He took another swig of whatever the liquid was inside of his flask and handed it back over to me.

"Do you know why I don't hate them, Ellis?"

I shook my head violently, trying to rid myself of the burning sensation that had settled on the insides of my cheeks, as much as I was disagreeing with him.

"Because they are men, just like us. A lot of them haven't seen their home for many months. There's nothing that they want more than to be able to go home, just as we do."

He looked at me for an acknowledgement, as I simply sat stunned, trying to process what this battle-hardened and combat experienced man was saying to me.

"I've been away from home for as long as I can remember, fighting wars that seemed to have no real consequence to me and my family. And all I pined for when I was there, was home. But, all I could do was follow orders, and pray that soon, I'd get to go back home. That's how they'll be feeling just over there. Remember, they are humans too, they're just following orders."

"Yes, Sarge," I croaked, still stunned by what I was hearing.

"Their orders are to kill you though, Ellis. Yours are to kill them. That's all there is to war. It is actually quite black and white.

"Do you know what makes a man into a good soldier, Ellis?"

I shook my head, like I was a young lad once again, doing everything my father told me to do, in case he got the leather belt out for another go.

"Recklessness. That's what makes a good soldier, above everything else. You have to care about nothing, not even yourself, to become a good soldier. But to become reckless, you need to let go of hope. That's why I know that you *will* be a good soldier, Ellis. You're still holding onto your hope, you still think that you might make it out of here alive, but you can't think like that."

"Sarge," was all I could mutter to him, but his harsh whispering wasn't over yet.

"Don't worry, something will happen to you which will make you let go of your hope. Then you will be able to kill, then you will be able to fight back. That's when you'll get the respect of men like Etwell. Alright?"

"Yes, Sarge," I spluttered, as he packed his flask away and tapped me on the knee.

"There's a good lad. Don't let it get to you, it was your first time out. We all get it."

He left me to my own devices, as he slowly made his way around all of the others who were still awake, offering each of them a sip of his paraffin, in between his own gulps.

I did not know whether to feel buoyed or thoroughly depressed by his little speech. It had comforted me a great deal that a man of his experience and stature had recognised something in me, that my quietness and timidity had not been mistaken for any kind of cowardice or fear, but rather out of a desire to be better.

It felt good to know that I had someone that was there looking out for me, and one that seemed to know exactly how I felt. I wondered what he had meant by 'we all get it,' toying with the idea that when he had first been into battle that he too, had made a mistake, that had ended up with another man dead. Maybe that was what had helped turn him into such a fine soldier.

On the other hand though, I began to feel completely downcast and annoyed at the sergeant for his advice. To tell me that I must lose my hope was something that I had never expected to hear, and I couldn't imagine how it would have made me a better soldier.

Surely I was able to become an effective infantryman, whilst still retaining my desire to stay alive? But, maybe I couldn't. I couldn't tell, my head was all over the place.

As I rubbed at my head, to rid myself of the thumping headache that I had taken possession of since Needs had left me, I realised that the thumps weren't in my skull but were, in fact, just outside the trench.

"Incoming!" screamed Etwell as the first few crumps of unmistakeable four-two shells began to hammer down into our position.

The air was suddenly filled to bursting with shells falling from every possible angle, making me breathe in huge chunks of earth and dust, stirring up an incredible thirst as I did so.

I, along with all the others, buried myself in the parapet, hoping that it would offer some sort of futile protection that you would not be able to get elsewhere.

I yanked at the sides of my cap, hoping to pull it down and over my ears, to block out some of the awful screams of the shells as they hared towards me.

Large chunks of dirt and rubble began to pitter patter down onto the ground around me, splitting into a thousand smaller pieces when they connected with my skull.

"I told you they'd be on their way soon, didn't I!" hollered Beattie, as I caught sight of his face grinning back at me not fifteen inches away from where I was pressed into the wall.

Shells fell from the sky like they were never going to end, the sheer crescendo staying at a constant volume for what felt like hours. I wondered how much longer I could stomach the incessant nature of the noise, as I felt myself slowly going insane from the constant torture that it was putting me through.

Suddenly, just as I thought I wasn't able to take anymore, there was an almighty wallop, followed by a roaring of air as the pressure wave expanded, obliterating everything that lay in its path. I felt the sandbags above my head immediately tear through the air, thwacking into the far side of the trench as they lost all their momentum.

For a few seconds, I was thankful for the close call, as I went completely deaf, the crumps and scrapes as shells landed and things were thrown around becoming completely non-existent for a few seconds.

My hearing returned, just in time to make out the first of the screams, as a roar of flames suddenly licked over the top of the trench further down the line.

"Everyone, heads up, heads up. It could be an advance!"

From the short time that I had been in the line, I had come to expect an enemy attack at dawn, not at four thirty-five in the morning, when it was still dark. But, then again, I had also learnt that there were no rules on the frontline, anything goes up there.

Reluctantly, I grabbed my rifle, not knowing whether I'd actually be able to fire it if I was called upon to use it. Straightening my cap, in preparation to meet the enemy, I plonked my rifle down hard on the top of the parapet, my sandbag-less portion of the frontline now being significantly less protected than the rest of my section.

A great, rolling mist was all I could see directly ahead of me, the darkness and manufactured fog rendering me more or less completely blind.

The curtain that had been pulled right across our frontline was unwearyingly renewed, as shell after shell continued to pummel the same sections of earth, never deviating from the same holes that they had attacked last time.

I wondered for a moment if it was being done deliberately, and that the Germans merely intended to put us off from another advance later on in the morning, before I concluded it was far more likely that they had got their aiming slightly off.

I prayed desperately that the German spotters were just as blind as I was, so that they wouldn't be calling any corrective fire, more accurate fire, down on us anytime soon.

The flashes of blindingly white light were tremendous, and for what felt like an age, I almost forgot that we were still in the grips of a wintry morning darkness, as each roll of thunder was quickly accompanied by a horizon-illuminating lightning.

Suddenly, just as I was blinded by yet another flash of brilliant white, a figure came thundering into our section, while the shells finally began to fall less frequently.

"Direct hit! Help, there's some of them buried!"

Needs suddenly sprang into action, "Beattie, Etwell, Harris, get back on your fire steps, keep a look out for any movement. If you see anything, pop them. Ellis, Sargent, you're with me, let's go!"

Looking across at Bob, we mirrored one another, as we slid our rifles away from the frontline and hopped down from the fire step. We weren't given a chance to prepare ourselves for what we'd see.

7

By the time that we had made it to the dugout, the private who had called out to us was already in floods of tears.

I hadn't noticed it when I first laid my eyes on him, but as we arrived at the scene, I realised that his uniform was all ripped and torn, a by-product of being so close to the initial blast site. Blood gushed from his head, faster than he could dab away at it, so he simply let it be, dribbling from somewhere underneath his hairline, and following his jawbone, before dripping from the end of his chin.

The young private's blood was the only blood that could be seen upon making it to the direct hit site, everything else being so strangely clean that I began to think that the poor fellow, who stood beside me crying, had been making the whole thing up.

"You're from number three platoon, aren't you lad?" queried Sergeant Needs, obviously recognising the crying private.

"Yes, Sarge," he managed to squeeze out, in amongst the sobs as he tried pull himself together, "Private Shaw, Sarge."

"Okay then, Shaw, I need you to go back to our dugout, get yourself patched up. Hold it together now, there's a good lad."

From the look on the Sergeant's face, I realised that it was one of compassion, but also one of slight disgust, clearly disappointed with Shaw suddenly breaking down in the way that he had.

As he scarpered off, the sergeant stepped aside, to reveal the full force of what had happened, so that Bob and I could see.

The trench seemed to carry on as normal, the boards, that had been put down to help avoid trench foot, ran right the way up to around the centre of the dugout, before they simply stopped.

The walls of the trench seemed fairly intact, the sandbags still perched patiently on the parapet, observing the scene of destruction below.

There was only a small part of the wall that had been disturbed, and had now cascaded, like some sort of landslide, into the main body of the trench, filling a lot of it up so that it was difficult to see the other side.

From the very bottom of the congregated earth, I could make out one, solitary hand poking out, as if it was somehow gasping out for air. My instincts were to simply reach out and grab it, but there was something holding me back, preventing me from wanting to help.

"Can anyone hear me?" called out Sergeant Needs, quietly at first, before raising his voice to ask the question a second time. He got no response.

Slaughter Fields

"Right lads," he said to us, taking on an air of practicality and coldness. "There's going to be bodies in here. They're going to be dead, but we still need to be careful, take our time. No entrenching tools. Just our hands. Move the earth gently but quickly."

We were soon scrabbling around, redistributing the disturbed earth and pulling it away from the mound that lay all around us.

The first body that we uncovered, about half way down the pile, was a complete mess, his chest opened up as if a surgeon had just been about to start some sort of major operation on the bloke. His uniform was no longer a khaki colour, but a deep brown, perfectly dyed from the collar of his shirt, right the way down to the very sole of his boots.

Sergeant Needs and I grabbed under his arms, gently trying to avoid any unnecessary ripping to his limbs that might cause the poor fellow even more discomfort, with Bob gripping a hold on his ankles.

We moved him clear of the rubble and set him down, pulling a German blanket over the top of him, to cover him from any further exposure.

The body was immediately ingrained in my mind and, as we began to excavate even more of the collapsed trench, I realised that every body that I saw was slowly becoming less and less apparent to me. Each one seemed less of a human being, until I was practically throwing the bodies around, without a single thought for what they might have been like when they were alive.

One of the bodies however, was gripping tightly onto a single, silver metal spoon, that I noticed had three numbers imprinted on the handle, possibly part of his service number or even his birthday. I found myself trying to forget the spoon, as it had led to a gateway of imaginings of what he had been doing moments before the shell had struck. He had been getting ready, I presumed, to tuck into some of his rations that he had been looking forward to for hours. Now, he would never get them.

"Right, that's all of them," announced the Sergeant, mournfully. "You two, take watch here, I'm going back to headquarters, seen if I can scrump together some replacements, maybe even a few stretchers if we're lucky."

He scurried away, his boots thumping down the boards as he left the two of us to fend for ourselves.

"You okay?" Bob muttered to me as we heaved ourselves up onto what was left of third platoon's makeshift fire step.

I couldn't answer him for a few moments, as I tried my hardest to scan the pitch-black landscape before me, hoping desperately to see a dreamlike world, one that was full of green grass and maybe even a cow or two, just anything to distract myself from what lay a few yards away from me.

A couple of the blankets that we had managed to throw over the bodies were beginning to become soaked in blood too, the volumes with which the bodily fluids had begun seeping out of the corpses, becoming unimaginable as soon as we had disturbed them.

I felt bad for them, not because they had been killed, but because they were going to have to have a second burial, the ground upon which they had fallen deemed far too important to have let them stay there.

A few minutes later, the sergeant returned, with the remainder of our depleted platoon, announcing that fourth platoon were being moved up from the reserve as we spoke, to take control of our dugout.

"Poor gits," announced Beattie as the bodies were dragged onto stretchers ready to be buried in some mass grave somewhere, "didn't know what was going to hit them."

"I reckon that's how I'm going to go, you know," sighed Harris, as he started to light up a ciggy and offer them round.

"What, waiting for your elusive rations?" smirked Beattie.

Harris gave a weak snort, the kind that someone gives at a slightly distasteful joke. Beattie knew immediately that he'd said the wrong thing and began to drum his fingers on the top of his rifle out of uneasiness.

"Give us one of those would you?" I was surprised to hear myself utter the words, as was Beattie, but he chucked the small cardboard packet towards my face, which I caught with an expert hand.

"Keep the lot," he said, as if he wasn't quite sure that I had converted or not, and he was expecting me to chuck the packet back at him in rebuttal.

"Told you!" cried Bob, triumphant that he had managed to finally get me onto them. "You two both owe me some money!"

He shot an accusing, but half-hearted look at both Beattie and Harris, who both began to hold their heads in shame.

"That's if we live long enough to be able to claim our

pay," called out Harris, now striding over to me to have the honour of lighting my first cigarette.

I felt the smoke envelope my nostrils to begin with, before I felt the burning sensation float down my throat and encompass my lungs. It tasted foul to me, and for the life of me I couldn't understand why these small things were such a popular commodity in the trenches, but it was taking my mind off the events of the hour before, and so, soon after finishing my first, I sparked up a second.

As I finished the last cigarette in the packet, the others finding it eternally funny that I had become so hooked on them so quickly, I began to meander on the image of the poor lad clutching hold of his spoon.

He had been expectantly waiting for his rations, not even imagining for a moment that he might not get them and had died in the half a second it had taken for a fluke shell to land on his head.

As I pictured his body, his sorrowful, mournful eyes that were locked in a desperate eternal glare, I came to the conclusion that it had all been down to luck. I had never been one to believe in fate or chance before but, in that moment, I decided that was all that it could possibly come down to.

He had been sitting in his section of the trench and I in mine. Both of us had been eagerly awaiting news of our rations and when we might be able to fill the hole that was in our bellies. Both of us had been sat on the fire step, surrounded by the rest of our platoon and what we could safely say were the best friends that we had ever had.

It just so happened that the shell had landed directly in his dugout, and not in mine.

I wondered if this was what Sergeant Needs had been on about when he said that to be an excellent soldier you had to let go of your hope. I was coming to the realisation that there was nothing you could do, nowhere you could hide that would guarantee your safety in this hellish war.

For all I knew, the spoon wielding solider could have been a veteran of many of the empire's campaigns, it was even possible that he had taught others on how to fight and survive in the trenches. But all it had taken was one shell.

I began to feel slightly better as I reasoned with myself that it wasn't because I was a terrible soldier that I may end up dead, but just down to a bad draw, being dealt a bad hand.

I took a quick look around our dugout to scan the faces of the other members of my platoon. For the most part, I couldn't make out who they were, apart from when they inhaled on their cigarette and I caught a glowing apparition of their scared, timid faces.

None of them seemed to ooze the confidence that I had expected of a British soldier. When I had marched off to war, even when I had stridden into the trenches for my first experience of being on the frontline, I had been brimming with an assurance that had managed to convince me that I would be the best soldier that there had ever been, and one that was guaranteed to make it home safely.

I was going to be different to everyone else. I was going to be careful, I was going to weigh up the risks of everything that I did and make sure that I made it through alive.

But, as I looked at their forlorn expressions, it became

apparent to me that, out of all of us, the one that was most likely to be killed was the one that was expecting to live. In amongst all the bombs and bullets, it was the one that was focused on getting home, and not on getting the job done, that would end up with a mouthful of dirt out in No Man's Land.

I began to see my cold, lifeless body out in No Man's Land. A tall skinny figure that had been so weak physically that he had only just made it through his infantryman training, his face planted firmly into the mud caused by the never ending whizz bangs. As I did so, I finally began to prise some of my fingers from the element of hope that I still harboured in my heart.

It would never be gone completely, I told myself, but I had loosened my grip on it all the same.

"We're all going to die here," Etwell suddenly began to grumble, and I wondered if he realised that he was actually speaking out loud, and if he meant to be saying these things to himself or not.

"The brass are utterly obsessed with death and watching things explode. There is no way that we're going to make it through the next few days. Mark my words, they'll have us marching on that village before too long...They've given the Hun enough time to set their guns up there perfectly. Have you noticed how it's never straight away? We could have taken that village while they were all still in a confusion. But now? They'll be dug in better than before, and they'll be expecting us."

We all sat in a cold stone silence, as the dying embers of Etwell's cigarette were tossed into a puddle of muddy rain water, that was now infused nicely with a decent helping of sticky blood.

A Very light suddenly kicked off behind me, taking me by complete surprise. I knew I shouldn't have done, but I couldn't stop myself from peeking up over the back of the trench, onto the illuminated battlefield that we had advanced across nearly twenty-four hours before now.

All I could see was a mixture of mud and bodies, some of the branches and wooden ornaments that scattered the land, still smouldering nicely, even after all this time. There was nothing there that had seemed worth taking, not even a nice row of flowers that had somehow managed to survive the onslaught, it was just mud.

From here, I could quite easily see the well sandbagged parapet that had been our frontline the day before, not five hundred yards away from where I now stood.

The rest of the division, as far as I was aware, had taken a right basting at the hands of the Germans; unprotected flesh, against the might of machine guns and well-aimed rifles. Five platoon had become so depleted that we had now amalgamated to form a single section, and I wondered if before too long, the whole division could be abbreviated into a single company, or maybe even worse.

The Garhwalis, the Indian soldiers who had advanced on our flank, had also been decimated, cut to shreds by the waiting machine guns and I wondered if they were feeling how I was right now.

We had taken less than five hundred yards of ground, which had consisted of nothing more than a barren landscape, torn apart by the never-ending ordnance that both sides had poured on it. The land was good for nothing, there would be no way that any kind of crop or cattle could make use of it for some time, so why had we taken it?

We must have lost thousands of men, up and down the line, during the advance, and I couldn't see for what reason we would have taken it. The Germans had been perched in their trench and we in ours, and we had been perfectly happy taking the odd pot shot at one another, maybe even killing a man here or there, but we had felt relatively safe.

The Very light glared in the night sky, brighter than the sun ever could, and I avoided looking at it directly for quite some time. The groans of the wounded out in No Man's Land had slowly died away as time had gone on, as they either passed away or simply gave up on their dreams of making it back home, or even the frontline.

The bright landscape suddenly died out, as quickly as it emerged, as the Very light gave up, withering away before it struck the ground in a silence.

It took me a few seconds to regain my vision, and before too long, I was staring at the ghoulish faces of the men of five platoon, all of them simultaneously striking their matches, to meet with the objects dangling from their mouths. I followed suit.

Harris must have sensed that the mood was beyond desperate and began trying to make optimistic noises, humming a tune for two or three seconds, before coming to a stop.

"Anyway," he said, sounding almost gleeful, "I've heard that they're developing a new shell that can deal with the Hun's barbed wire, even better than if we struck the factory making the stuff."

He looked around for our approval, clearly hoping

that we would suddenly start jumping up and down, clapping and cheering at the news. But all he got was the gruff, depressive tones of Etwell.

"Well, I hope they remember to fire them a few hundred yards further ahead now. Knowing our luck, we'll get one straight on our noggins."

8

We continued the monotonous cycle of smoking, taking watch and sleeping for what felt like days, but in reality, wasn't anything more than a couple of hours. It was only just approaching six in the morning. I had been awake for over twenty-four hours.

No one seemed to say anything, apart from the odd grunt at one another to take over on the fire step, or to take a peek over the top with a periscope that the sergeant had managed to nab from somewhere.

We had been informed that sandbags were on their way to us soon, as well as a Vickers that we would be able to set up to better defend our section of the line. I imagined the top brass and the quartermasters sprinting around, trying to find anything and everything that we could use to consolidate our position somehow. We were all having the same thoughts, so it didn't come as too much of a surprise when one of us sparked up a random conversation.

"I tell you what would help to shore up our position

here," grumbled Beattie, his cigarette bobbing around furiously within the grips of his lips.

"What's that?"

"All them brass hats up there, the ones that are meant to be commanding this horror show, give them a rifle each. It might do them some good to see what things are really like for us. Plus, I reckon there's at least a few hundred of them up there, that could plug a gap in some of our losses. What do you reckon, Sergeant?"

He turned his head to Needs, as he came off his imaginary soapbox.

"I think," Needs began, "that someone who wants to become an NCO needs to switch his filter on. There's a time and a place for saying certain things. The brass will be doing all they can."

I wondered for a moment if Needs actually believed in his own words, or if he was as dejected as the rest of us, merely trying to lift our spirits slightly in the face of everything that had happened.

"Oh, my filter is well and truly on, Sarge. There's plenty of voices in this old head of mine that don't make it out into the open."

Beattie got a few nervous chuckles, but for the most part, they were short and polite, a blip of happiness before being dragged straight back down into the depression that was looming over all of us.

"The engineers are beginning to build a connecting trench from our old frontline, lads. Trying to consolidate our position."

"What's taken them so long to get started? Couldn't work out which end to dig with their tools?" Beattie was on form all of a sudden and a few more, involuntary chuckles began to waft their way around the trench, from men that had nothing to be laughing about.

But he was right, we had taken this trench by eight in the morning yesterday, and it was now five thirty in the morning the following day and they were only just getting started.

In my heart, I knew why; the brass had been expecting some sort of a counter attack by now, one that would have quite easily overwhelmed our boys and forced them back over No Man's Land. I wondered how much longer it would be before that was the case.

I couldn't help but imagine that by this time tomorrow, the Germans would be back in their trenches, and what was left of us, back in ours, hopefully so far behind the line that we would practically be back at home.

Everyone had more or less silently agreed it as fact that, by this time next week, the Germans would be back in their trenches, thankful to the British troops who had merely improved the defences somewhat, without them having to lift a finger.

The idea of a German counterattack was one that was weighing heavy on my mind, a burden pushing strongly on my back. I had been thinking, ever since we had settled in this trench, when the next occasion might arise that meant I would be able to prove myself to the other men, to stop them from thinking that I was weak.

As I searched myself, I was fairly confident that I hadn't let go of all of my hope, maybe just loosened my grip on it slightly. There was still a part of me that kept imagining home, continued to envisage what it was like and even what life would be like for me after the war had ended.

I didn't believe what Needs had said to me was the whole truth, I still maintained that a soldier still needed *some* hope, a reason to dodge the bullets and shells, and have something to look forward to, to aim for.

But, I supposed as another Very light kicked off somewhere down the line, the only way that I could find out if my loosened grip was enough, would be to throw myself into another advance, towards the spitting machine guns and abusive rifle fire, which is exactly what Etwell was convinced was going to happen.

"They'll be getting their rations soon. Fighting on full bellies they'll be. Bet they ain't short on ammunition neither. Or men for that matter."

Etwell was a special kind of defeatist, a fatalist even. But what he was saying felt like the truth, everything that came from his mouth seemed to slot in with the facts that were all around us; the lack of rations, the depleted state of manpower and the way in which it had taken the brass so long to sort things like sandbags and machine guns out for our defences. It really did seem like everything and everyone wanted us dead. It was a hole of thinking that I could see absolutely no way out of, until maybe the war was definitely over.

Just as Etwell finished the latest of his snippets of good news, Captain Tudor-Jones, one of the poshest men that I had ever met, suddenly made an appearance in the trench. Tudor-Jones was of a fine stature, a chiselled, clearly defined face that had matched his crystal-clear accent. It was almost like he hadn't just been born into the aristocracy, but purpose-built for it.

Despite what could have made him a natural target for the likes of us, he was well respected and liked by the vast majority in the company, apart from one or two, like Etwell, who seemed like he would hate his own mother had he known her.

"Good morning, boys," he announced chipperly, as if he was about to tell us that the war was over, and we could pack our bags to leave.

"Hello, Sir," came the altogether less enthusiastic reply.

"Got some news for you all. Good and bad. Good news is reinforcements are on their way up here as we speak, first battalion of the Grenadier guards if I remember correctly. They'll take over the central sector of this line, which means we'll be pushed further over to the left flank, mixing in with some of the other battalions who are already there." He looked at us for some kind of reaction, which he didn't get, apart from one or two cigarettes glowing away in the gloom.

"The bad news?" It was the question that was on all of our lips, but only Harris had mustered up enough courage to ask and find out what it was.

Captain Tudor-Jones wasted no time at all in relaying the news to us. "We're going over, again. We're taking the village that the Germans fell back on yesterday. The village itself is built around a series of crossroads. The plan is that we advance until we get to the first set of crossroads, whereupon we will break away to the left of the advance, to try and flank the Germans. RFC boys reckon that there's a machine gun holed up in the ruins of the church there. From up in the skies they reckon it could be the difference between success and failure. It is our job to take it. We will essentially be the protecting force for the rest of the division.

"Either we'll take the machine gun ourselves, or at the very least, draw its fire away from the rest of the division."

"So, we're just the worm at the end of the rod, sir?" Beattie was matter of fact and blunt, with no emotion in his voice whatsoever, not even a hint of the continuous sarcasm he normally harboured.

"To put it bluntly, yes. But you're good men, excellent soldiers. If there's any platoon in the whole of the division that will succeed, it will be you chaps."

Beattie suddenly thrust a packet of cigarettes under the nose of the Captain, who obligingly took one, as he awaited the inevitable barrage of questions that would soon be heading his way.

"Thank you, private," the Captain said, as I watched Beattie almost wince in pain at the failure to identify him as the acting lance corporal title that he was so proud of. The rest of us sniggered and stared at the ground, as Beattie went about lighting the cigarette for the Captain.

"Sir," chimed in Harris, as soon as he had calmed down from the hilarity that was Beattie's sudden demotion, "why are they sending us at all? We're not exactly at our full strength."

"I know, I know. But you lot form the bulk of the advance, the core around which we can put faith in. I'll make sure you get some rations to you as soon as possible, get your strength back up a bit."

I couldn't quite tell if he was trying to be funny or not, but either way I supposed that we would have to be grateful for the meagre rations he would source for us, even though a tin of condensed milk would find it more difficult to fire a rifle than an eighteen-year-old replacement.

Silently, we all seemed to accept what the captain was saying, an element of pride even slipping in that we seemed to be trusted by the officers who were again sending us into battle.

"Sir, the other thing is we can't…well…we don't have a CO, Sir," I wondered whether Harris was somehow trying to get out of the advance, by throwing up as many obstacles to our effectiveness as was possible. Part of me thought that the captain would soon be arresting Doug for desertion, before he'd even managed to escape the trenches.

"Of course you do," Tudor-Jones scoffed, his face lighting up with glee that someone had brought the issue up. "You've got the sergeant here. He's your new CO… Well until you get a replacement to relieve you of your command, sergeant."

Sergeant Needs nodded knowingly to the captain, as if he had been here a thousand times before already. The truth of the matter was that Needs had effectively taken command of the platoon even when Fairweather was still alive, as he nurtured both the new recruits sent to the frontline in the form of Bob Sargent and me, as well as the inexperienced, young and naïve officer who was his senior in rank only.

There seemed to be a mutual appreciation of one another between the captain and Sergeant Needs, and I got the distinct impression that they had known each other for a while, and that they could depend on one another to do their respective duties. I wanted to ask both of them what they had experienced together, to glean at least a shrapnel of wisdom on being a good soldier, but I refrained.

Slaughter Fields

"One other thing, sir," my voice, crackled and weak as I tried desperately to clear it, to sound as grown up and manly as was possible. "Why are we waiting? We could have carried on straight after the advance yesterday, now all we've done is give them time to organise themselves."

The captain seemed impressed at my question, not least because I was an eighteen-year-old volunteer who seemed to be thinking tactically. For a moment, I saw myself as a general, who would outmanoeuvre and outwit the enemy each and every time we went into battle. Maybe one day, I thought.

"Good question, private..."

"Ellis, sir."

"Private Ellis. The reason is so that our friends over in the Field Artillery are able to resupply their guns, to support our advance. That way, they can deliver an almighty barrage which means there will be practically nothing left of the Boche by the time we get there. We wouldn't want to go in without the big guns, would we?"

"Oh, absolutely not sir," Beattie began to blurt, the sarcasm in his voice undeniable. "I've always wondered how something that can make so much noise can be so ineffective."

"Bit like you then, Beattie," cut in Harris, as quick as flash, which got him the pleasure of a cigarette butt tossed in his direction.

"Anyway," announced the captain, for a final time, "if there are no other questions, I'll be off. I'll get food to you soon, maybe even a little rum. Hold fast gentlemen."

No one bothered to salute him as he disappeared, even I had learnt not to alert the possible German marksman to who was more important than who and where they were by now.

"So, we're the flanking movement," Bob began, "aren't they the ones that always end up dead?"

"You're learning young Bobby," Beattie grinned. "They want us all dead."

9

Within half an hour of leaving us, Captain Tudor-Jones had come up trumps, with a team of his orderlies arriving with armfuls of supplies, in truth too much for such a small section that we now were.

I threw the coffee down my neck first, its lukewarm and rather lumpy consistency completely ignored by the fact that it had been the first thing that had stimulated my taste buds for twenty-four hours now, having dealt with the monotony of water and cigarettes for the last few hours.

I felt eternally grateful to him, despite the fact that I had always got the impression from the others that anyone above the rank of a lieutenant was bound to only be in the army for their own gains.

Even if that was the case, Tudor-Jones was the subject of all my gratitude and happiness that morning, and I felt particularly lucky to have him as my company commander for the time being, until, that was, he would end up dead, just like the rest of us.

He was only about twenty-two or three, but he had experienced this war right from the off, being one of the first men in the BEF to set his boots in France and seeing what kind of a conflict it was going to be from the first few skirmishes of the war. He had been bandied about as he had been promoted, taking up various different commands to impart some of his experience and wisdom to some of the other, invariably elder but less experienced, officers that littered the whole of the army.

I wondered if he had let go of his hope, in the same way that I was meant to, or if he could picture himself as getting back home and living an ordinary life. I supposed that the life that he would be going back to would be vastly different to my own, the aristocratic and landed gentry circles far more prolific and enjoyable than what would await me if I was to return home.

I had surrendered my employment upon joining up for the army, and I doubted that I would ever get it back again, if the look on my uncle's face was anything to go by when I had told him of my plans. Tudor-Jones on the other hand, would return home, his servants still at his beck and call for any of his daily needs, as he went back to his game hunting, or maybe even entering parliament.

But, for now, in terms of our lives, we were equals. There was no discrimination of a marksman's bullet, no deviation to the less fortunate when an artillery shell landed. In this war, both officers and other ranks were dying, those related to royalty or those related to pig farmers. Everyone was susceptible, and to me, the thought gave me an element of comfort.

As I flicked the last of my post-coffee cigarette away in between the wooden boards of the trench, I pulled the

Slaughter Fields

small can of bully beef in towards me, having saved the bulk of my supplies to the end, giving myself something to look forward to, however meagre it was.

I began to attack the can, ripping and tearing at it to get to the meaty treat that was captured within the tin walls.

As I opened the tin fully, I looked up for a fleeting second, realising that, for the first time in a while, I was actually feeling happy. I knew that within a few hours I would be marching towards the spitting machine guns, but, for now, I wasn't, and if I had learned anything in the last twenty-four hours, it was that a soldier's life was to be lived in the here and now, not worrying about what might lie ahead, because you might not even make it that far.

Etwell, as ever, had volunteered to go on watch, as if for some reason he didn't trust any other man to spot the enemy out in No Man's Land. In reality, he simply didn't trust me or Bob Sargent, the two newest recruits who had only joined up for a little jolly to Europe.

The rest of the platoon were dotted around the section of trench that we had made our own. Rifles were leaning up against walls, all perfectly spotless, which was more than could be said for the state of our uniforms, which were now caked in a thick layer of drying mud, that had begun to flake off in large sections like dinner-plates, but left an unmistakeable twinge on our kits.

I was at the extreme left of the trench, my feet up on a wooden crate so that I was looking down the hallway that extended out slightly in front of our trench, leading to the other section manned by another platoon.

I was quite content to sit there, on my own, feet perched up on a box while I tucked in to my delicious feast courtesy of the captain, and I was sure that the others too could sense that was the case, and so left me to it.

Sargent, Beattie and Harris sat on the fire step, playing a game of cards that I had tried and failed to learn the rules of a few days ago, mugging each other of their wages before they had even seen a single penny of it. Beattie kept a small book in his top pocket that kept a record of who owed what to whom.

Sergeant Needs had disappeared to receive more detailed orders of the planned attack, as our new commanding officer. As I looked at my watch, I realised that it was approaching twenty past six, and guessed that he would be back before too long, to prepare us for a dawn attack, probably at seven thirty.

Suddenly a sound filled my head, as if someone behind me was taking in an abrupt inhalation of air, the sharp, prolonged hiss being the only thing that I could hear, the only thing that I could really focus on.

As I was tossed through the air, like whatever hand had thrown me didn't care about me in the slightest, I felt everything in my body go completely numb. In an instant, I didn't feel like I had any arms or legs, and that I was just a brain, that was floating around somewhere in the trench.

My eyes were tightly shut, but I could make out a wonderful, bright, red-orange glow right on the other side of my eyelids and for half a second, I felt almost peaceful.

I realised that this must have been it for me, that the lucky shell had fallen on the unlucky section of the front-line and I was the poor little soldier who was going to cop

Slaughter Fields

most of it. I was almost certainly about to don my wooden overcoat.

My mind suddenly switched to where my burial site might be, if there was going to be enough of me to bury, and whether or not my family would be able to visit my grave someday. I hoped that they would be able to.

As the numbness began to wear off, I realised that I could feel all of my limbs, I could wiggle my toes and curl up my fingers. In the same second, I noticed that I had come to a stop, I was no longer cartwheeling through the air, but I was resting on something, something solid. I had landed.

Still convinced that I was dead, I began to think of my grandfather and whether the next face that I saw would be his, as I had missed him so terribly since he had died some years before.

But as the pain began to develop, like someone had bitten into my upper arm and were sinking their teeth in further and further, I decided that I must have still been alive. Wounded maybe, but alive.

The sinking teeth penetrated my skin further and further as the final few remnants of numbness faded into nothing and all I could feel was the pain in my arm.

I could hear nothing, apart from my breathing, which was so infrequent and sporadic that I may as well have been dead already. I supposed that the artillery shell that had flung me through the air had attacked too my eardrums and that I should settle for being deaf for the next few minutes at the very least.

As I lay there, I realised that there was no point in me trying to work out if I could sit up or move or not, as I knew that I wouldn't be able to, a decent helping of provoked earth was already pressing down firmly on my chest, and I knew that if I was to move, it would likely do more harm than good. For now, I would wait, and hope that no one else in my trench had been unlucky enough to get hit.

The only thing that I could do to try and keep myself alive was breathe, which is what I focused on for the thirty or so seconds immediately after I had come to a stop. Surprisingly, the pain began to subside for a moment, as I managed to find enough air in my makeshift grave to steadily calm myself down and work out what my next move was going to be.

I began to make out faint thuds on the outside of my kingdom, and recognised them as the infuriating shells from the Germans that were carrying on, quite ignorant of the fact that they had got me.

The crumps and deep pops as the other shells obliterated anything within its reach grew louder and louder, until I could, very faintly at first, begin to make out voices that were screaming with all their might above the din of the artillery barrage.

It was difficult to make out what it was exactly that they were saying, but by their tones, I could make out that they were worried, desperate almost and I began to wonder what it was that was wrong. I thought maybe the trench had taken multiple hits, and the bedraggled platoon that was now nothing more than a section, was maybe now nothing more than two men armed with rifles.

The possibility crossed my mind that the Germans were beginning to counter attack and, at the thought, I tried to manoeuvre myself as best as I could, trying to locate my rifle so that I could join in the defence.

I was too weak however, against the piles of earth that pressed down on me with a fierceness, so much so that I resolved to lie there in wait, for rescue, for death and anything in between.

"Got him! He's here!" I couldn't tell whose voice it was, but the fact that I could hear it, filled me with an immeasurable amount of joy that I was about to be rescued.

I felt a hand resting on the side of my head as he called in to the rabbit warren he had created, "It's alright Andrew, we're going to get you out!"

It was Bob Sargent, the only one who had seemed to understand what it was I was going through in the light of my first piece of action the day before.

I tried to mumble back a response, but succeeded only in taking in a small mouthful of dirt, which I forced myself to swallow down, to stop myself from suffocating to death. By now, the air was warm and plagued with so much moisture that it felt like I might drown. At the thought, my breathing began to get more erratic, as I desperately craved the fresher air of what lay on the outside of the rubble.

It didn't take Bob too long to pull away at the dirt around my head, so that I could breathe with an element of normality. Even the air out there, thick with smoke and death that had been produced by the falling artillery, was more welcome than the fresh seaside air that one could take in on the shores of England.

Two pairs of hands suddenly gripped just under my armpits, my right arm burning up in a fireball of pain that rushed the length of my arm as they did so. Tugging me out of the dirt, I realised that Beattie had been helping in the rescue efforts, although no sooner was I out, then he had turned and made off in a direction which I could not see.

"You're alright mate," gasped Bob as he tried desperately to get his breath back, leaning over me to protect me from the falling dirt that was now raining down on us.

Beattie suddenly returned with an aid kit, getting to work instantly on the piece of shrapnel that had come to rest in the top of my arm, right by the shoulder. I winced as he ripped it from its hole, feeling the skin tear as easily as a sodden piece of paper.

"Sorry, mate. Got to be done." He carried on patching me up, before slapping me quite unsympathetically just above the wound, which was just as tender as the hole itself.

"There ya go, good as new."

It was then that I realised that this was as close to death as I was probably going to get, without the eternal silence that would follow if I was finally going to cop it.

What could I have done differently? Maybe I should have endeavoured to have learned the card game, that way I would have been on the far side of the trench, and would have escaped with nothing more than a pounding headache. Maybe I should have been more attentive to the situation around me, maybe then I would have heard the shell before it had landed, giving me some more time to react.

As I dwelt upon it some more, I realised that there was nothing that I could have done and resolved myself to thinking that the shell hadn't killed me for a reason, maybe it had just been a warning.

The picture of home was slowly changing, morphing into one where maybe I didn't exist. If being blown up had been down to anything that I had done, I would have ventured to change it, to make myself more alert. But there wasn't a thing to be done, it was all down to luck. That and the fact that it seemed like no one was going to survive this war.

I felt depressed, like I had lost the one thing that had set me apart from all the other dead men in this hell on earth. And then the depression got even worse.

"Bob…my bully beef. It's gone."

10

The rumblings of my stomach, the ones that had mourned the loss of my bully beef, had been put to bed, courtesy of the other men's generosity, as I was allowed a mouthful of each of theirs to satisfy my hunger. The price I'd had to pay was the constant teasing throughout, the nickname Bully Beef Ellis apparently being hilariously funny, so much so that it began to stick.

The pain in my arm too, was not so bad, especially after Sergeant Needs had entrusted me with his flask, filled with his paraffin, that had started to numb the pain from the third or fourth sip onwards. I felt bad that I had it, as I tossed it over and over in my palm, and wondered what his wife would have said, if she was to find out that he had simply handed it over to a foolish young soldier, who had managed to get himself blown up.

They couldn't evacuate me to an aid station, as I was needed in the advance and for once, I didn't actually want to leave the frontline. I felt like I had a duty of care to these men now, the ones that had managed to dig me out and share their rations with me, I wanted to fight alongside them.

Almost as if they had been in retaliation for young Private Andrew Ellis, somewhere on the frontline with five platoon, the Field Artillery boys began to chatter back with the guns that were some way behind the German frontline, smashing the ground in front of us to pieces, and hopefully that machine gun nest that was settled nicely in the church.

As I poured some more paraffin down my neck, burning everything that it came into contact with, I wished sincerely that it would numb my hearing once again, as well as the pain in my arm. The blood curdling screams of Satan's own personal hell hounds as they howled overhead were truly harrowing, as if he had called in his attack dogs to kill as many as possible and drive the remainder totally insane.

The ground trembled almost as much as my knees were doing with every sorrowful impact the shells made into the earth up ahead. I felt like my major organs were going to give up on me at any second, being shaken so much that I couldn't imagine how much more they could put up with the abuses.

I wondered how quickly the Germans had risen from their beds as soon as the first shell had landed, throwing themselves behind the nearest cover that they could find.

"Oh, why are they doing that?!" screamed Harris as he gave up trying to sleep and sat up right on the ledge that had been his bed. "Keeping the Boche awake is fine, but they always forget it keeps us up too!"

He was shouting with a great intensity, just to be

heard above the din, but even then, he was as quiet as a fish in water.

Even though it was shaking me within an inch of my life and it was keeping an irate Harris from getting any rest, I was still ever so slightly grateful to the sheer amount of ordnance that was being dropped on the Germans' heads.

There were so many shells, each one bursting not half a second after the previous one, that had it been daylight, I was sure I would be able to see a blanket of steel as it flew through the air towards the Hun.

Even if they weren't going to be doing any real damage to the German defences, it felt quite nice to at least semi-believe that we hadn't been totally forgotten. Even the officers thirty miles behind the line knew that to send us in without any kind of visible support would lead to nothing short of an all-out mutiny.

Feeling that my apprehension was going to reach boiling point, I felt around in my breast pocket for the small talisman that I had kept in there, ever since I had left for France.

It was a large, heavyweight coin that my father had carried around during his time in the South African republic. It felt good in my hands and comforted me to know that, in some way, my father was with me on the frontline.

As I turned it over and over in my hand, switching between the front face, declaring it was a penny and the back, that housed a profile of some bearded man whose name I could no longer remember, I wondered if my father had ever been this scared.

I began to think back to his tales of war, to recall a

minor detail that might have exposed how he was feeling. But there had been nothing, not even a mention of how his mates and comrades had been feeling at the second before an attack. As ever, although I felt close to him, and to those who were sitting around me, I felt completely alone in my thoughts of despair and fear.

I popped it back into my pocket, making doubly sure that the button was fastened before it fell out somewhere in No Man's Land. There was one thing that I had remembered about my father's experiences of war and that was the way that he, and the rest of his comrades, had questioned why they were even there in the first place.

For them, it was a colonial war that was not worth fighting, it was one that was completely unwinnable. To them, there was no one army that they were fighting, not one cohesive group of individuals all coordinated and administrated from a central location. They were fighting the Boers, the men who had begun to split off into smaller groups, ambushing trains and army patrols in the most barbaric ways possible.

As I watched boneshaking tremor after soul-crushing quiver in the side of the trench wall, I began to question why we were really here, why *I* was here.

For the life of me, as I searched myself, I couldn't think of a single reason as to why this war was happening, as it had seemed so far removed from my place in society, it was almost as if I hadn't been worthy of knowing why we were here. But then, I realised that I was doing it for those around me, I was doing it for men like Sargent, Beattie, Harris and even Etwell, to give them some meagre chance at survival, so that it wasn't their loved ones that would receive a telegram to say their son wasn't coming home.

We had all signed up at some point or another, for the sake of duty, like it had been the duty of young men for generations before us to defend our nation and what was right. It was just my turn, that was all.

That's where a lot of the soldiers that I had met had continued to take their strength from, in that ill-fated notion of for King and country, for the sake of national pride and standing, only to have all your ideals and beliefs blown out from your skull and painted down the side of the trench with a single sharpshooter's bullet.

I realised that, as the shells continued to howl overhead, that I was increasingly taking my courage and my strength not from some pathetic idea of patriotism, not even from the man that would stand next to me, but from the bottle, in particular, Sergeant Needs' bottle.

I sipped away at the awful concoction until it no longer burned my throat and nostrils, but merely warmed them, gently. The more I drank, the safer I felt, the better I felt.

But I was gripped by a guilt that even the Germans weren't entirely deserving of the thousands of pounds of bombs that were limply falling from the sky and onto their positions. They were doing it for the same reasons that we all were, and I was certain that more than one or two of them wanted nothing more than to pack up and get on the next train back to Germany.

The others found it so easy to hate the Germans, particularly Etwell, but I was finding it increasingly difficult. The average soldier was merely following his orders, in the same way that I was, and I wondered what the chances were of either of us wanting to kill one another if we were to meet outside of the trenches, outside of this war. I had no desire to kill a man unless he was pointing a rifle at me, probably the same as him. Which meant we could have been in an endless stalemate until one of us gave in and lowered his weapon.

As the thoughts continued to tumble around my mind, I realised that I was crying, great baubles of water launching themselves from my eyes and thumping into the ground with as much of an effect as the artillery shells.

No matter how hard I tried to stop them, even poking my fingers into the tear ducts themselves, there was nothing I could do to prevent them from splashing all around me. Before too long, I had given up completely, allowing the tears to carve themselves a route through the grime and dirt that was all over my face, before eventually washing my cheeks over with the accumulated dampness that was on them.

I rubbed my eyes for the hundredth time, trying to pull myself together and not let anyone else see that I had been bawling my eyes out through the barrage. When I lowered my hands and opened my eyes again, I caught the large, imposing silhouette of Etwell, as he strode his way towards me, aggressively.

"Pull yourself together! You are weak! You are nothing!" he spat on me as his words tumbled from his mouth, wounding me with more of an effect than a German machine gun.

"This is an industrial war! We have been sent here to die! The sooner you accept that fact the better! There is *nothing* you can do! Nothing!"

My face burned ferociously as I recoiled from the slap that he had delivered expertly across my cheeks, before he gripped them tightly, forcing me to stare straight into his eyes.

I had expected to see them burning a bright red colour, as his anger and malice towards me reached new levels. But all that I could see in his eyes was a sense of resignation, like he knew that he would die, and so would everyone else. There was an emptiness to his expression that told me he hadn't had the life that he had wanted, hadn't even experienced the same things before the war that many of us had, and I immediately wanted to know what it was that was missing from his life.

For the first time since I met him he spoke, still in a shout to be heard over the screaming shells, but somehow softer, some might have even classed it as compassionate.

"It is nothing personal, Ellis. It is just the way it is." I was astounded with the way that he had spoken to me. I had known him for almost a month, half of that had been spent living in very close proximity to one another, and not once had he called me by my name, in fact he had barely spoken to me directly at all.

As if it had somehow taken all of the energy in the world for him to have said that, I gave him a brief, curt nod, my head still in the grasps of his sweaty palms, out of a thankfulness for his strange way of imparting his experience and knowledge to younger soldiers.

Immediately, he turned away from me and, as I wiped the final few tears away from my eyes, I felt somehow changed, like I didn't really care about the shells anymore, I didn't really care for the German soldiers on the other side of our trench. It was almost like I truly believed that they deserved everything that they were getting, for the first time in my life.

I looked at my watch. It was six fifty-three, ack Emma, A.M. It wouldn't be long now before the order was given to make weapons ready and to fix bayonets. It was nearly showtime, and I couldn't have felt better.

I grew impatient with the shells as they continued with their insanity-inducing wails, each and every shell that was launched over our trench just ratcheting the levels of anxiety that were present within our trench, inch by inch.

But for me, although I was nervous and scared, I felt like I had a renewed energy, from the pits of my stomach, and it had come from the most unlikely person in the platoon.

Thanks to Etwell, I had let go of all sense of hope. I wasn't going to make it home, and the realisation that it was true, had made me feel infinitely better.

11

There seemed to be far more smoke in our trench than if a German shell had just landed slap bang in the middle of us all. Every single man in that hastily dug hole in a French field, now bolstered with reinforcements from some men from the Grenadier guards, had something smoking away from the corner of his mouth, one or two even chucking up the pungent smells of a pipe as they puffed away on them.

As for me, I couldn't even remember what it was like to have never smoked in my life, having made my way through so many of the things in the last few hours, that I must have more than made up for the few years that the others had all been smoking for.

Sergeant Needs continued to keep a watch on all of us, checking for the tell-tale signs of an impending waterfall of tears, or maybe even the first movements of a deserting soldier.

All the while, he continued to scribble away in his notebook, that he balanced nimbly between his thumb and forefinger, flapping away as he wrote down line after line of whatever it was he stored in there. I wondered if it was everything that was zipping through his mind, as if writing it down would help to make sense of them all, or maybe it was his observations and recommendations for the soldiers under his command. I even toyed with the idea that he was heavily into his poetry and that he thought the tough exterior that he possessed would somehow be damaged by the revelation.

"Rum! Rum!" came the call from a man that was clearly making his way up and down the line spreading a meagre drop of happiness amongst the troops waiting to die.

The private appeared with a large jar tucked under his arm, as he struggled to carry the thing in his tiny little arms.

"Mugs out gents! Double rations this morning, courtesy of Major Barber!"

Mugs were hastily produced out of thin air, each man necking the thick, dark liquid so quickly that they barely had time to taste the stuff.

But, taste the stuff they did, and the men who received the ration before I did were already coughing and spluttering long before I had been poured my allocation.

"Blimey!" rasped Beattie, as it appeared that he was fighting for breath. "What on earth has he put in that stuff!"

"I told you," gasped Harris, clutching at his throat as if he had been poisoned, "they all want to kill us!"

I swished the muddy like liquid around in my cup before I reluctantly drank it. The thought occurred to me that the rum was meant to give us an element of courage before leaping over the sandbags, but felt that, if that was to be the case, then the British Army should be far more liberal with their helpings than this young private had been, even if they were double helpings.

The thick, oil type liquid slowly trickled its way through my mouth and down the back of my throat. Even though it was strong, it wasn't quite as bad as my first taste of Sergeant Needs' paraffin type amalgamation, and so, in some ways I quite enjoyed it. At the very least, it managed to stave off the headache that I had been experiencing for the last couple of hours or so.

"Stand back, move!" came a call from over on my left, and I turned just in time to watch Bob Sargent drop his trousers and squat nervously in an unoccupied corner of the trench. He groaned and grimaced as he left his bowels all over the back of the trench.

"Eugh," groaned Beattie, with an element of laughter tinging his voice, "you've got it all down the back of your trousers."

"Dirty pig," chimed in Harris as his accomplice.

"Shut up," strained Sargent, "it's not my fault."

He wasn't the only one who felt the need to relive themselves at a moment's notice, with several others only adding to the horrific aroma of human excrement, vomit and sweat that lingered in the air like a poison gas.

Others couldn't help but shuffle around, like I was, trying to ignore the pains in my bladder, passing them off as merely down to a fear, one that would soon pass as the excitement of the advance would surely take over.

The remainder of the occupants in the trench did nothing at all, except for simply staring at the walls with an intensity that made me think they could look straight through them. They wore blank, faded expressions on their faces, their skin so pale that they looked like a freshly laundered bed sheet that was being hung out to dry.

There was nothing anyone could do for any of them anymore, there were various ways that men tried to cope with the fear, and that was their chosen method.

I glanced down at my wrist watch and I watched as the second hand sped up for a moment, before it slowed right the way down, to the point where it was barely moving any longer. Seven twenty-six. Not long to go now.

I found myself staring at my watch, as if I was transfixed on the way that it seemed to be counting down to my death. I willed it to stop completely, to give me some sort of a respite from the torture of being made to wait, while in the same second, I urged it to speed up, so that I could get over the sandbags and get whatever was about to happen over and done with.

I was distracted by Sergeant Needs sidling up next to me, as he tucked his notebook away in his breast pocket, tapping it gently.

"Oh...Sergeant," I muttered fumbling around in my own top pocket, "I forgot to give this back to you."

"Keep it," he growled, with a wink, "I'll take it off you on the other side. But you're paying to have it refilled."

I smirked at him weakly, as I struggled to see the funny side of his joke. He must have picked up on the sheer terror that was in my eyes as he sighed, staring straight at me.

"Oh, come on, now. It was just a joke, Ellis. Besides, I

know that you're going to make it through, I'm confident of that."

"You really think so?" I responded, still maintaining my new-found belief that thinking you're going to make it through does nothing but distract you from the task at hand.

"Yeah..." he said, drawing it out so that it sounded more like a belch than a word, "I've seen far worse soldiers than you making it out alive, Ellis."

I pondered his words for a second, "But seen far better ones killed?"

He smirked at me, turning his head back towards the ladder that was propped up against the wall, awaiting us to clamber up and over it.

"Just keep hold of that flask for me, would you? Keep it safe, now."

It was at that moment that I realised someone was talking, and for a moment I thought that maybe it was me, and that I had gone completely mad and had started talking to myself. But the voice was not one that I recognised as my own, it was Harris.

He was clutching hold of a small, battered and browning book that fit snugly into the palm of his hand, his dirtied fingernails digging in hard into its spine as he clutched it. His eyes were clamped firmly shut and his head was tilted to the sky, as if he was worshiping the falling artillery shells.

But it wasn't the deity of artillery that he was praying to. He muttered his dreams over and over, interspersed with several repeated seconds of, "Please, Lord. Please. Please. Please..."

Slaughter Fields

I stared at him for a moment or two longer, my eyes beginning to fill with tears at the sight.

"For my comrades...keep them safe. Keep *them* safe, even if you don't keep me safe..."

No one seemed willing to stop him from his mutterings, even if they didn't believe. It just felt good that someone was there that did, making me anyway, feel slightly more confident now that we had God on our side.

As I scanned the faces of the rest of my platoon, I caught sight of Bob Sargent kissing his ring finger, despite the fact that he wasn't even married, and I wondered why he had done it. Maybe he was married, but he had failed to tell us, or maybe it was on the promise of an engagement if he was to make it home that had made him do it. Whatever reason, I left him to it, I didn't want to pry at a moment like this.

As for myself, I felt momentarily for my father's coin, as if it was going to bring me some sort of relief, but as I gripped it, I realised it would do nothing for me. I found that I was getting far more comfort from the faces that were around me, the pale faces, the ones that had the faint dribblings of vomit in the breath, the ones that were crying and the ones that were praying earnestly. I wasn't the only one to be feeling scared. I wasn't alone in this.

I could almost hear the watches ticking up and down the line now, and as I looked at my own again, I noticed that we had made it into the final two minutes before the advance. Seven twenty-eight.

Flicking my head over to the other side of the trench, I observed Beattie, as he suddenly dropped his rifle to the ground, as if it had some sort of electric current passing through it. He whipped his cap off, and began to run his hands through his hair, licking at his muddied palms before wiping down at varying tufts as if his life depended on it.

"Beattie, what on earth are you doing?" queried Needs, picking up on his antics at the same time as I had done.

"Doing my hair, Sarge. You never know who we're going to meet over there. I need to make the right first impression!"

"You really are one obsessed fool," chuckled Needs as he turned to face me, his eyes rolling comically. I smiled half-heartedly back at him, before readjusting my gaze to stare back down at my wrist.

One minute left to go. Seven twenty-nine.

As I looked around at the sweating, tearful faces, for what I presumed would be the last time, I noticed something about them all. They were all fatalists, each one of them utterly convinced that they were going to die and, for the most part, it was a fate that was generally accepted. But each one of them, in those final few seconds before the push, still had a small ember of hope in the back of their minds. Maybe one day they would get home.

At the very least, not one of them looked like they were ready to die, not one of them looked like they wanted to die.

Thirty seconds to go.

The quaking legs and the shaking hands, some drumming nicely on the side of their rifles, seemed to intensify somewhat, to the point where they almost rivalled the noise of the artillery that was still zooming overhead. The

Slaughter Fields

closer we got to the agreed time, the more intense the little quirks became.

"Okay then, gents," bellowed Sergeant Needs, a slight tremor even in his, experienced voice. "Fix bayonets!"

The chimes of bayonets being drawn from sheaths and slotted onto rifles made the trench sound more like the battle of Agincourt than the Western Front, and it acted as a reminder to myself that I was petrified, my fingers dancing all over the place so that the bayonet struggled to click into position.

Eventually, I got there, just in time to check my watch one last time, before pulling my rifle up and off the top of my boot, where I had been resting it to keep clean.

Twenty seconds to go.

Needs shuffled around to my left and drew out a sparkly little piece of metal.

"A parting gift from the Captain," he said, this time without a wink and altogether far more solemnly.

I gave him a nod, just waiting for the whistle that he played with in his fingers, to give off the shrill scream that would signal our advance.

I felt sick to the very pit of my stomach as I watched the final few seconds tick by, a cool sweat suddenly rolling down from under my arms. My hairs all stood on end.

As the second hand hit twelve, I noticed that the final dull crump of artillery seemed to sound at just the right moment, before nothing. That was that then. The generals had done their bit. The field artillery had done theirs. Now it was just down to us.

I looked up from my watch face to be met by the sergeant's, as he raised the whistle to his lips.

He blew down on it hard, and repeatedly, in case someone, somewhere wasn't able to hear its harrowing battle cry.

He broke our gaze and turned away from me. My heart thumped. I gripped the bottom of the ladder.

12

My kit weighed heavily on my back as we began the slow walk towards the village, in silence. Nothing seemed to stir for the first hundred yards or so as we moved as one, long line and I wondered for a moment if a ceasefire had been called that we hadn't been told about.

Up ahead, I could make out the perimeter of the village, which was still smouldering after the artillery that had hammered down on them a matter of minutes ago.

We marched across the field, the approach road that led to the crossroads suddenly appearing out of nowhere over to my right. It looked odd, the cobbled stones that led into a small village totally devoid of any life or buildings.

We knew that they were still there, they simply had to be, it was just that we couldn't see them immediately.

As the swishing of footsteps continued to march through the mud and small patches of grass that had, until very recently, been the reserve lines of the German trench system, I wondered how much longer it would be before the Germans suddenly opened up.

If it was me, I would be waiting with all the machine-guns that I could muster, and let as many soldiers march upon me as was possible. Then, at exactly the right moment I would order everyone to open up, to inflict as much pain and destruction on the approaching forces as possible. That's what I was supposing was going to happen in that village.

"Remember lads," Needs hissed to us all, "take those crossroads, we've got the village. Help those boys get to the crossroads."

Immediately after the sergeant had finished speaking, almost as if they had been waiting for him to finish his little monologue, every machine gun and rifle in the whole of the German empire seemed to spark up, chattering away between one another as they pinged darts all around us.

I heard the three distinctive cracks of a machine gun sparking up somewhere over to my left, before the three rounds were kicking around at my feet, throwing up dust and dirt in equal measure. Every fibre of my being wanted to throw myself to the ground, hoping that the lie of the land would help cover me in some way, but I knew too well that all it would do would turn me into a fantastic target for the Germans.

I could almost feel the operating handle cranking itself forwards and backwards as round after round was sent shooting from the end of the barrel towards me.

As the sounds of bullets tearing through human flesh began to reach my ears, mixed with grunts and screams

Slaughter Fields

of wounded and dying men, I realised that it wasn't just the one machine gun that had opened fire on us.

From where we were, there was one on the right flank, over the far side of the crossroads, with another one positioned in the centre, that had an excellent field of fire straight down the approach road. I supposed that other teams, similar to ours, had been tasked with neutralising those threats, and so tried to wipe them from my conscious mind as best as one can when they're trying to cut you down.

It was the one on the left flank, the one that had spat three bullets at my feet, that I was most preoccupied with. It seemed to be sat quite snugly in the ruins of an old church, with only one wall that could be identified as being a building of prayer, all the others lying around the gun in large chunks, the size of footballs.

The piles of sandbags all around it was the main giveaway that there was something there worth protecting, that and the fact that an eruption of noise was emanating from within its defences.

That was the machine gun placed on the Germans' right flank, the one that would be waiting to cut down the troops once they had made it to the crossroads.

That was our machine gun.

"Find cover! Get behind something!" screeched Needs, as the bullets began to make a spectacular impact on our small raiding force.

I leapt behind what must have once been the corner of a house, just as some more bullets thwacked into the concrete on the other side. I tucked my legs in and clutched my rifle to my chest, convinced that what I was hiding behind was far too small to really hide me properly.

A few more rounds whizzed past me on either side of my tiny bit of cover, one round catching a poor boy behind me straight in the kneecap. He threw his rifle from his arms as he collapsed onto the ground before him, screaming in agony. Within seconds, he was crawling his way towards me, his eyes fixed on mine as I sat there silently watching him, willing him to make it to me so that I could drag him behind the remnants of the wall.

Just as he lifted himself to heave his broken body closer to safety, three soft pops resounded, blood bursting from his chest as the rounds pierced his skin in an upwards motion. He stared at me for half a second longer, his head shaking gently as he steadied himself after the impact, before he slumped forwards into the ground, motionless.

"Ellis! Where are you! Let's move!"

The screams of the sergeant made me snap out of my trance, as I heaved myself away from the cover and bounded towards the stone water fountain, that still stood defiantly, by the edge of the road.

Needs was squatting behind it, his head scanning behind him for anyone else that might have been left behind who could lend a hand. I could make out Beattie, Etwell and Sargent with him too, each one of them lying down behind the stone structure trying to forget what was happening.

Needs must have screamed at them to do something shortly after I poked my head out from the wall, as each of them popped up, firing off rounds in the general direction of the machine gun, doing nothing to slow their rate of fire, but at the very least ignore the figure that was charging across open ground to get to his mates.

As I flew across the ground, I caught sight of a body, one that I recognised. It was Harris. He had been pinged right in the face, not in the forehead like one would imagine, but he had taken it through the nose, which had left a huge crater in his face that made it look like his nose had been ripped clean off. The only way that I was able to identify him was by the small, browned, leather bound bible that was still clutched in his palm.

I forgot about him as quickly as I had laid eyes on him, as I threw myself into the stone fountain, just as great shards of it were being ripped off by the rounds that were now keeping us all pinned down.

"Nice of you to join us, Ellis!" screamed Beattie, who was grinning from ear to ear as he had slid back down to push more rounds into his Lee Enfield.

"Harris is dead!" I blurted, not really thinking of the consequences for Beattie, who had been particularly close to him.

"They want us all dead!" was his defeatist battle cry back to me.

"Be of use, Ellis! Come on!" Needs was hollering directly into my ear now, as a few explosions kicked off to our right, hopefully as the second and third machine guns were overrun.

I swung my rifle up onto the top of the small wall, which could only have been shin height if I was to stand next to it properly. I realised that the small bath tub of water that it housed was scummy and covered in an almost undisturbed layer of dust, the water shaking gently with every vibration that erupted from the machine gun.

I fired off four rounds, before more bits of ancient stone was flicked around in my vision, causing me to duck back down behind the comfort of the wall, with everyone else.

I realised that it was the first time that I had fired my rifle in action before, and I hadn't even given it a second thought.

"That's the first time you've fired, isn't it!" roared Beattie, as he looked across at me with eyes wilder than a rabid wolf. "We all had it! Everyone gets that look in their eye!"

The machine guns continued to rattle away incessantly, but I struggled to hear too many rifles kicking off in amongst the battle, the lack of their higher pitched cracks so noticeable that I wondered if the Hun had any at all.

It concerned me to see that the machine gun was so heavily defended with sandbags, but no other positions were, which made me suspect that the main bulk of the German force had already evacuated. But I merely put it down to wishful thinking, the Boche wouldn't simply give up on a village such as this, especially as it was so close to the railway lines that they depended on for supplies.

"Over there! Can you see that building?" Needs hollered, pointing in the general direction of a pile of bricks, which once must have been a schoolhouse, owing to its close proximity to the church. "That's where we're going, we should be in range to do some real damage there!"

"Sargent, Beattie, Etwell! You're up first. Head down,

as fast as you can! We'll cover! You ready, Ellis?" he bellowed, turning to face me. I quickly pushed another charger clip into the bridge, before pushing them down forcefully by pinching them securely.

I forced the bolt forward, flicking it down expertly, before I looked back at my sergeant, and nodded.

"Right boys...Move!"

As soon as he had uttered the words, I was kneeling behind the wall, my sights set at around two hundred yards, aiming just above the heads of the Germans that I could see peppering our hiding place.

I fired off three rounds rapidly, each time feeling the cocking piece slam forward to eject the round, with each empty cartridge sent spinning way off to my right somewhere with every heave of the bolt.

Just as I was lining up to take my fourth shot, I caught sight of Sargent, sent cartwheeling over to his left, as a round entered his body. A gasp passed involuntarily over my lips, as I pulled the trigger without really looking at what I was firing at.

Without letting himself stay on the floor for too long, Sargent pulled himself back to his feet, his left arm dangling down limply from the rest of his body, blood gushing from his elbow leaving a trail of scarlet liquid behind him.

Within about five seconds, I was completely out of rounds, as was the sergeant, but the others had already made it to the schoolhouse, and were now setting themselves up to cover our approach in towards them.

"You ready, son?" Needs said as he finished reloading his rifle, watching me go through the final few motions of doing my own.

"Yes, Sarge!"

"Come on then, let's go!" I let him go first, following close behind him, but leaving enough of a gap that I wouldn't be cut down in the same burst of fire.

He was slower than I was, and I found myself catching up with him as we charged our way towards the others, their rifles kicking and bucking as we slowly made ground and closed the gap between us.

The machine gunners were really having a tough time to keep up the incredible rate of fire that they had been, as the three rifles in the schoolhouse continued to pour well aimed and rapid rounds down towards them, so much so that the sergeant and I could quite easily have strolled towards them, without a single machine gun bullet coming our way.

"You alright, Bob?" I shouted, sucking in more dust and smoke than oxygen, as I tried desperately to catch my breath.

"It's nothing!" he returned, without turning back to me, rounds still flying from his weapon as he spoke.

All of a sudden, the machine gunner somehow managed to traverse the gun round, so that it was able to fire on us with a pinpoint accuracy, even though he too was under heavy fire.

All five of us hit the deck as quickly as we could, as large sections of the wall gave way to the bullets that thumped into the only solid cover that was nearby.

Several of the others swore and I flinched as a shard of brick landed forcefully on my stomach.

"Where's the rest of the advance?!" howled Needs, as he started to desperately look down the road for some kind of relief.

As the machine gun stopped to reload, Etwell and Beattie began to empty the remainder of their rounds in the direction of the church, while the rest of us scanned the village for any sight of another British soldier. But we could see no one.

It was almost as if we had been left totally alone.

13

"Where are they! Where on earth are they! They should have moved up ages ago! They should be by that gun now!"

I had never seen the sergeant ever raise his voice in this way before. Of course, I had heard him shouting many times, but never in the flustered and panicked way that he was screaming as we lay in the ruins of the schoolhouse.

Just as another volley of bullets zipped over our heads, I could make out the second machine gun, the one that was situated in the middle of the crossroads, momentarily turned our way, inaccurately pinging some rounds in our direction, but spitting them in our direction nonetheless.

"How are they firing on us?!" erupted Etwell, and I felt sorry for the bloke who was going to get the blame for it later on. "They should be engaging them! That gun shouldn't have the time to be firing at us!"

It had only been a short burst, but that was all that it

Slaughter Fields

had taken to tell us that something was seriously wrong with the bulk of the advance.

"We're going to die here, if we don't do anything, Sarge!" called out Bob, who was now hastily trying to wrap a dressing around his own arm, with little success. I managed to shuffle my way over to him, tying it so tightly that he almost began to cry, while Needs began to mull everything over.

"Ellis, how fast are you feeling?"

"Like the wind, Sarge."

"Right, okay. I need you to fall back, go back the way we came. Find an officer, any of them, and find out what on earth is going on with those guns. Then, bring some men back with you if you can, we're not getting out of here on our own."

The others had heard what he had said perfectly, and began loading in their charger clips of .303 rounds into their rifles before he had even finished. They were ready to leap up, in the face of the oncoming bullets and give covering fire to the fool who was about to expose himself in the open once again.

I puffed my cheeks out sharply, "See you in a minute then," I said, trying to find something of a grin from somewhere, but could only muster up a slight twitch of the lips.

As soon as I had said it, I leapt to my feet, my legs creaking and cracking as I did so. I began to focus on the small stone water feature that I had been crouched behind not five minutes before, and I felt greatly encouraged by the sheer scale of the noise that the rest of my section were able to direct towards the machine gunners.

It was only when I was half a yard away from the

fountain, that the bullets began to chip away at the masonry, by which time, it was too late, I was safely behind it.

Grazing my chin on the floor as I threw myself to the ground, I took a few seconds to try and get my breath back, focusing on where I would be running to next. Never once did I look back behind me to see how the boys were getting on, as I was confident that they would continue to have my back, right down to the very last round in their rifles.

I barely waited for my own breath to catch up with me, instead opting to get the whole charade over and done with, jumping to my feet and charging towards the small corner of wall that had been my solace earlier on.

The machine gun was either totally surprised that I was still alive, or they were too engrossed with the handful of rifles in the schoolhouse, as not a single round seemed to be aimed in my direction. Still, it didn't stop me from clutching onto my cap as I ducked and ran.

The boy that had been caught through the knee was still lying there, face down in the dirt and I quickly scrabbled over to him, tugging the bandolier that he had over his chest and relieving it of his possession by passing it over his head.

The cloth bandolier was almost full, which meant that he had close to thirty rounds of spare ammunition that he would never get to fire. Hopefully I would.

I felt almost safe as I began to weave my way through the rubble of the village, the big guns still booming further ahead, but too distracted by the presence of other troops to be dealing with a lone threat like me.

Eventually, making my way to the main road that led

Slaughter Fields

into the centre of the village, I came across a young looking lieutenant, hiding behind the rubble of a building on the far side of the road.

He copped me, immediately stopping me from crossing with a firm hand.

"Wait there! As soon as you step out, you'll be cut down!"

I didn't need to be told twice, and so stood there staring at him as he mustered some of his boys to lay down some fire for me.

As soon as the first round kicked out of their rifles, I was practically on the other side of the road already, a hail of bullets taking half a second too long to readjust and bury themselves in their target.

"Who are you?"

"Private Ellis, Sir. Five platoon. We're on the flanking movement to take out that machine gun on our extreme left. Problem is, Sir, is that we were told you would be moving up the middle, taking the fire from the central gun, but we're taking it all. We need help."

The lieutenant stared at me for a moment, and I thought for a second that he was going to punch me as I had accused him of failing in his duties.

"The flanking team on the right are completely gone, that's the gun that's firing on us here. I've sent some more men to take it, in the hope that they draw its fire and free us up to take that gun. How many men have you got over there?"

"Five, including me, Sir. One of them is wounded."

"Okay, hang tight there a second. Wait for the gun on the right flank to open up on the new team, then take these three men with you and we'll begin to advance as best we can on the central gun."

"Sir."

We didn't have to wait very long before the gun on the right flank began to fire away at something in their line of sight, acting as our starting pistol to begin our charge over to the left flank.

"With me!" I screamed at my new command, a group of three men who looked even younger, and more frightened than I was.

We leapt over bits of rubble and dodged bullets, until we came to a stop at the water fountain again. By the time we had made it there, I was down to just two men.

"Over there," I said, flicking my palm in the general direction of the schoolhouse, "that's the rest of the platoon, we're taking that gun. Do you reckon you can deliver some well-aimed shots on the gunner?"

I got a curt nod from the two of them.

"Right then, I'll move up, tell my sergeant what's going on. Hopefully you can knock out the gunner while he fires on me and my mates."

They were pretty good shots. Within five paces of the water feature, the machine gun had begun to chip away at the cobbled streets around my feet, as I expectantly waited for the sinking teeth feeling again as a round or bit of stone embedded itself in my flesh. Within five more paces, the gun had momentarily fallen silent.

By the time that I had made it to the schoolhouse however, the gun was rattling away again, like a rabbiting vicar who couldn't be deterred.

I found a rifle pointing square in my face and for a

moment I braced myself for the explosion of pain as I was executed by one of my own.

"Who are you?!" screamed the voice, drowning in tears and pain.

"Beattie?" I queried, "It's alright mate, it's Ellis."

Blood was pouring from his head and trickling down it from an invisible source on the top of his skull, his eyes bloodshot and apparently bruised from some sort of impact. He had gone totally blind. From the left side of his neck, he had what appeared to be an almighty splinter poking out from it, apparently only puncturing the skin but not one of his major veins, that throbbed even more in all the excitement.

"Where's Needs?" I found myself screaming, trying to get to my sergeant so that I could relay the news to him.

"He's over there!" came the hoarse reply, as Sargent bent down to take Beattie's rifle from his grasp, passing his unloaded one to him for Sam to blindly reload.

I looked over to where he had nodded his head and laid my eyes on Sergeant Needs, who was staring unceasingly towards the pale blue sky, as if he was watching the birds pass over his head. He looked quite peaceful.

Even from here, I could make out what had killed him, a large hole nicely in the front of his neck, at least two inches in diameter, where a round had passed through his throat and out the other side. He would have been dead in a matter of seconds.

His blood was sprayed all over the wall, and he must have been lying next to Etwell at the time, who had a decent dosage decorating the left-hand side of his face.

The blood was almost as copious as the cartridge casings that now littered the floor, and, at the thought, I tore the bandolier from my person and pressed them into Beattie's hand.

"There's some more rounds in there mate, keep loading them for us."

I laid down in the rubble, taking up position next to Bob Sargent and began firing slowly on the machine gun, which must have been close to expending all their ammunition.

"What's the situation?"

"The right flanking movement was wiped out. Right hand gun was firing on the centre of the advance, leaving the central gun to pick their targets. New flanking movement was sent to engage the gun, freeing up the main advance to come up the centre, they were about to move as I left."

We continued to fire repeatedly for a minute or two more, passing our rifles backwards towards Beattie, who was doing a fine job of reloading considering he couldn't see a thing.

"This is hopeless," I shouted above the din, "We're never going to be able to take the gun from here. We're going to run out of rounds."

"What do you suggest?" Etwell asked, sarcastically.

He was surprised when he realised I had an answer.

"Well, we need to get Beattie out of here for starters. I think falling back to that fountain will help for now. There's already two others over there, they can cover us. When we're there, we'll take stock of ammo and work out what we're going to do from there. That gun is not going to advance on us, is it?"

He knew I was right, and began to make movements to get Beattie up and ready to fall back.

Slaughter Fields

"Ready?" Etwell said, as he had Beattie's arm over his shoulder, ready to guide him to safety.

"Go," I announced, immediately firing a full complement of ten rounds towards the machine gun, in double time.

As soon as I had finished, I ducked down to reload, peering out towards the water fountain, where I hoped to see both Etwell and Beattie propped up behind the wall, introducing themselves to my new mates. But I was met with a sight worse than that.

Beattie was lying on his back, clutching at his chest as he leaked blood all over the cobbles. Etwell had been hit in the legs, and was trying to crawl to safety, as the Germans toyed with him by putting rounds either side of his body, as if they were deliberately trying to avoid hitting him.

Beattie suddenly rolled over, and I could make out the calls of the other two men, trying to guide the blind soldier in towards them.

Suddenly, his body convulsed, red rain suddenly scattering itself far and wide, as one of his hands was completely ripped from his body. For a moment, I was sure that he was still alive, his body twitching every second or so, before he came to a complete stop.

I looked at Sargent, knowingly. We both knew that we were going to have to make the charge sooner or later, and that our fate was as good as sealed.

Reloading our rifles, and flicking the safety catches forwards so we didn't accidentally shoot one another as we ran, I watched as Etwell was dragged by his arms, as he came within touching distance of the other two soldiers.

"Get back there, join the main advance?" Bob piped up. "Safety in numbers?"

"Sounds good to me, mate."

We smiled weakly at one another, before I noticed that the machine gun had suddenly stopped. Giving one another a nod, we leapt up, to run to the fountain before the machine gun was able to reload.

My joints felt like they were going to give way under the strain that I was putting them under, my mind even more fragile as I realised that I had left Sergeant Needs there without so much of a goodbye. At the thought, I touched my breast pocket, the flask was still there.

My trousers ripped as I skidded along the ground on my knees, ready to return fire the instant that we had made it to the fountain, but there was no need. The gun hadn't restarted, the chattering of machine gun rounds suddenly falling very silent, across the whole village.

For a moment, it was almost a perfect calm, apart from the agonising groans of Etwell, as he dealt with the two large holes that had splintered his shin bone.

Then, just as I thought the whole battle would be over, I made out a few low thumps, like a distant bass drum in a marching band, slowly waft down the canals of my ear.

I turned to look at Bob. He shrugged, dejected.

14

The Germans began to shell their own positions, after what had appeared to be a rigorously timed, coordinated retreat.

As the shells began to smash into anything that would put up some sort of resistance, I chanced a look down at my watch. It was exactly eight in the morning.

I quickly glanced over the top of the small stone wall, just in time to watch the sandbags over at the church explode in a cloud of dust and a wave of pressure that made my ears erupt in pain. Feeling like they were about to start bleeding, I slid back down and looked across at Bob.

"They're going to put us in the ground," he said, shakily.

"Yep. We need to move, and fast." As if it had been waiting for my cue, a shell suddenly burst not thirty yards from where we were sitting, as the German barrage advanced away from their abandoned positions, and began to have a go at the floundering soldiers that littered the village.

The ground shook tremendously, like a mini earthquake had suddenly rumbled from the core of the earth, doing nothing at all to steady my nerves or convince me that I might live.

"Fall back," Bob began to croak, "link up with the main advance. Then we might find someone over there that can tell us what to do."

"Good idea," I moaned back, glad that he had the brain power to make a decision that I was far too afraid to be making.

"What about 'im?" queried one of the soldiers that I had picked up from the lieutenant, nodding towards Etwell.

"We're going to have to drag him. Come on, let's go," I announced, trying to take control of our very desperate situation.

Etwell grimaced and let out a long moan as I picked him up under his shoulders, struggling greatly with the gaping hole in his shin that was now pouring blood everywhere, faster than a milk jug that had toppled over sideways.

We began to move away as one group, Bob picking up Etwell's right arm so that I had less of a burden to carry. The other two moved slowly, but efficiently, acting as our beacons on where we were headed and where we could stop for some cover.

With every second that passed by, the constant rush of air as another shell destroyed a small patch of the village, began to draw even closer to me, with one golf ball sized lump of concrete coming just inches from taking my ear clean off as it zipped past.

The two rifles were behind a low garden wall, watching our approach but, at the same time, making sure they weren't as near to the danger as we were. Without warning, Etwell's weight dragged me down, as Bob suddenly fell to the floor, clutching the side of his head, a gash dribbling blood down the back of his neck.

"Bob, get to cover! Go! Go!"

At first, I wasn't sure what he'd been hit by and for a split second assumed that it had been a marksman perched in one of the abandoned ruins, taking pot shots at the retreating soldiers as they ran past.

But then, as two or three other shells sent bits of concrete and glass in every direction, I realised that it must have been a bit of debris or shrapnel that had caught him in the back of his head.

He did as he was told, and I could make out one of the figures breaking from cover to come and pull Etwell along with me.

In the meantime, I changed my grip, ignoring the pain in my knees and the excruciating burning sensation in my chest, so that I would be able to drag Etwell alone. I dribbled and spat into Etwell's hair, grunting with exertion to make it to the only piece of cover that was left.

It can't have taken the young lad more than five seconds to reach me, but by then, it was far too late. An eruption of brilliant white light in my vision, told me all that I needed to know, as I felt the air rush through my hair and whizz in my ears.

I was cartwheeling through the air, for the second time

in a number of hours, this time the numbness I had experienced before completely ineffective. It felt as though my chest had been forcibly ripped open, a searingly hot branding iron being pressed into my skin as I descended. My arm, where the biting pain had been before, suddenly erupted with a renewed vigour, as if the pain was working in tandem with each other, trying to bring me to tears.

As I landed in a crumpled heap on the solid ground, my lungs felt like they had collapsed as I struggled to breathe. I focused on sorting myself out, before I was interrupted by Etwell.

Suddenly ignoring the pain altogether, I sat up and more or less immediately turned away from him and began scrabbling to the young lad who had been on his way to help me.

"Forget him! He's gone! Get into cover!"

The boy did as he was told, as the artillery barrage crept closer and closer to us all.

"Ellis! Ellis!" came the weak, rasping call of Etwell, quite clearly drowning in his own blood. "Don't leave me, will you?"

I looked at his body, the gaping holes in his right shin bone now looking like nothing more than a school yard graze in comparison to his left leg. The sinews of muscle and shards of bone that could be seen coming out of his thigh were a burningly bright red in colour, which matched the deep, sticky liquid that Etwell now found himself lying in.

His left leg was some way away, perhaps five or six yards to his left, surprisingly close to where his arm now lay solemnly, detached from its original owner. The whole left-hand side of his face was painfully burned, the skin blackened and bumpy from the sheer force of what had happened.

I knew that it was only the adrenaline and initial shock that was keeping him alive now, and that in a matter of seconds, he would pass out, never regaining consciousness.

He stared at me with forlorn little eyes, his pupils so dilated I thought it a wonder that he was still able to move them around. In that half second of a glare, he realised that he was done for and that it was game over for him.

He began to mutter something to me, so quietly in the din that I had to pull myself closer just to hear him. It took me a while to work out what he was saying, but I soon realised that he was merely repeating what he had screamed in my face during the artillery barrage some hours before.

"...personal. It was never personal, Ellis."

I felt almost bad for him, as he slowly lay there dying, in the most hellish of circumstances. I had always been under the impression that everything would stop if I was to go down, there would be no gunfire and no artillery consistently banging down around you. There would be a brilliant silence, maybe even a bird or two tweeting.

But, for Etwell at least, there was none of that, as shell after shell continued to rain down around us, until I finally thought that it was my time to leave.

"I'm sorry, Etwell," I managed to squeak out weakly, which was met surprisingly with a wry smile.

"Don't be an idiot, Ellis. Get out of here before you end up here with me."

The young lad who had scrabbled out from cover to

recover both me and Etwell had ignored my command, and was now helping me to my feet, at which point I felt like my left leg was on fire. Upon inspection, my trouser leg was soaked in a deep red colour, adding a flare to the otherwise monotonous khaki.

"Can you walk?" questioned Bob as soon as I had been heaved into cover. He was still clutching at the side of his head, this time with a clean dressing pressed firmly into it.

"Yeah," I croaked, trying to sound like the hero, when in actual fact I was terrified of what sort of an injury I had sustained.

Together, now just the four of us, we half-sprinted, half-hobbled to the edge of the village, where we hoped desperately to see a friendly face.

It took us a few minutes, but eventually we did see a friendly face, well, one that we recognised anyway.

I noted the tall, imposing figure of Captain Tudor-Jones, Two Company's commander, the man who had been to see us to tell us the good news of this wonderful advance.

Except, he didn't look as confident and sophisticated as I had seen him only an hour or two before.

"Blimey," muttered Bob when he laid his eyes on him, each one of us stopping in turn at the mere sight of the fellow.

Tudor-Jones was crying, not small reluctant tears that you might expect of a member of the aristocracy, but huge, overwhelming tears, the kind that make a man go blind momentarily before they drop to the floor.

Although there were tears in plentiful supply, it was not accompanied by crying of any sort, no loud uninterrupted sobs that one might expect to resound alongside those kinds of tears. But, I wondered, if he had been able to, then maybe the sobs would have come.

Tudor-Jones clutched at his face, just underneath his jaw, tirelessly holding it together with the rest of his face. It seemed so limp and uncooperative in his palm that I suspected that, if he were to remove his hand, it would simply fall to the floor. There was an unprecedented amount of blood dripping from the whole of his lower face.

"Shell landed right next to him. Shrapnel ripped through his lower jaw," screamed a young looking corporal as he caught us all staring at him. "Get a move on, we're falling back. Start making your way there now, if you want to live."

We all stood stock still, each one of us marvelling at the captain for a moment or two longer, while the corporal dashed away to find the rest of his men.

Remarkably, even though he looked like he was for the grave at any second, Tudor-Jones was still flinging his left arm around wildly, moving people around silently, writing furiously on a pad that was held loyally by his batman, who also had a bandage wound tightly over a bloodied eye.

Men ran up to him, waited for a moment, read what he had written before bounding off to direct the men that were beginning to congregate around the edge of the village.

Suddenly, he caught sight of the four of us and immediately began thrusting his thumb back in the direction that we had advanced, his order as compelling and forceful as if it had been bellowed across the parade square.

We wasted no time whatsoever in actioning his plan, and began to hobble back down the broken road, as more shells began to fall in and around our position, threatening us from every single angle.

As I leant on my new acquaintance, I realised that this was where I was about to die. Everywhere I looked, there were artillery shells bursting; behind me, to my left, to my right and, most worryingly of all, dead ahead of me, exactly where we were headed.

Men lay strewn all over the place, not all of them quite dead and most of them in our immediate pathway, each one of them begging for help and compassion to take them back to our lines. Others still merely asked for a round between their eyes, to speed up the inevitable.

I could see no way out, whatsoever. I felt like the ones who were already dead, were the lucky ones, and that those of us that were still making for safety, whether that was walking, limping or even crawling, were merely being funnelled towards an inevitable butchery that would result in an entire division being wiped out.

It was at that moment that I realised I had quite quickly heeded Needs' advice to me. I had no hope. I was going to die, and that was all there is to war.

We had lost a lot of good men, all in the space of an hour and somehow, it had been the two new boys of the platoon who had made it out alive, the ones that were looked down on in a way by the others, as we hadn't been professional soldiers like them.

In some ways, I felt proud of myself, but in others, realised it had been down to a pure luck that I was alive and, if it hadn't been for Needs sending me to link up with that lieutenant, then there was every chance that I could have ended up the same way that he had done.

I looked across at Bob, his dressing now so sodden that it was doing nothing to contain the blood, but still he kept it there, pressed firmly into the side of his skull. I wondered what the next few days, or even hours would bring for us.

It was likely, now that the Germans knew we had taken a battering, that they would be attacking us before too long, and it really wouldn't take them too much to break through our lines and send us back to our original frontline of the day before. We really had been through it the last day or so.

I wondered if we were to be immediately rotated off the frontline, or if we would have to wait for the reinforcements to arrive. Either way, I hope they didn't call five platoon into action anytime soon, as there was only two of us left now.

Bob locked eyes with me and managed to give a hopeful, tinted with forlorn, smile. His teeth were scarlet red.

15

The young captain who stood before me, the three pips on his wrist denoting his rank were as crystal clear as his face was. The difference between this man and everyone else in the trench, was the distinct lack of blood and dirt, that seemed to plague every other poor soul that had collapsed in the trench.

Bob passed another cigarette to me, which I took without a thanks or acknowledgement, as the captain continued to stare down at the two bundles of dirt and blood that were threatening to soil his pristine uniform.

"Sergeant George Needs?"

"Dead."

"Acting Corporal Samuel Beattie?"

"Dead."

"Private Herb—"

"Look mate, we've told you, we're the only ones left in five platoon. Robert Sargent and Andrew Ellis. Can't you just leave us be?"

The young officer looked his list up and down, scribbling away at names as we confirmed which ones had been taken from us and who we hadn't seen go down. In actual fact, we had seen more or less everyone killed, or at the very least, about to die. It wasn't a particularly difficult task for us to recall all of their circumstances, they were etched upon our minds.

Bob and I had no idea where to go; even if we'd had the energy to go somewhere, we would simply be forced into wandering aimlessly around, until someone picked us up. I felt totally helpless, and more than a little bit lost.

No one seemed willing to tell us to be in any one place in particular, only getting us to shuffle up and down the trench, to make way for another stretcher case, that would more than likely be another fatal in the next twenty minutes or so.

Neither of us wanted to move and, in the absence of having anyone directly superior to us, we settled in the trench that we had taken twenty-four hours previously, intending to smoke ourselves to death.

We had no one to tell us what to do; no platoon sergeant, no platoon commander and the last time we had even seen our company commander, half his face had been hanging off. Even if he lived, he would have been in no fit state to continue to order us around, especially when he had had the time to calm down and realise he was in an incredible pain.

For a moment, I found myself wondering if any of the officers in the entire division had survived, or whether they had all somehow sacrificed themselves for the good of their men.

Bob Sargent and I, were something of divisional vagabonds and there was no way that we were going to risk being shot for falling back to somewhere where we shouldn't have, so we decided we would stay put, until we were forced out of our resting place and hopefully onto somewhere a great deal more comfortable.

The medics of the Royal Army Medical Corps were doing a sterling job, as they tirelessly made their way up and down the trench, tending to the individual men's needs, without stopping for so much as a sip of water themselves.

They did what they could, making men comfortable and ensuring that they were warm, before taking the very same blankets and placing it over the corpses once they had slipped into an eternal slumber.

They were caked head to toe in blood and for a moment I wondered if one of them had been hit himself, judging by the flow of blood that dripped from the end of his chin, but he moved so quickly I didn't have time to work it out.

The Padre was making his way around all of the wounded, fulfilling his duties as both a spiritual guide, but also taking his turn in propping men up for a drink and also bandaging up their wounds. He was a man that I had greatly admired, as he had spent a lot of time with our section, especially as he had been the only man that Etwell had seemed to talk to without raising his voice at.

I wondered for a moment if I should tell the chaplain that the bloke who he had helped to write letters, was now dismembered a few hundred yards from where we were, but decided against it, more out of a fear for what he might do in trying to recover the body, than for his own morale.

For the first time since I had met him some two weeks

before, I noticed that the Padre was rather old, far older than any of the other boys in the trenches by a long shot. He must have been in his early forties.

I wondered for a moment about his family and if he had one waiting for him back in Britain. I wondered what his wife and children would have made of the notion of him going to France, particularly at an age and an occupation where he could quite easily have avoided the entire show.

I respected him even more as the thought slowly began to dwindle from my mind.

The dull thuds of artillery in the distance, shortly followed by the excitable gasps over our heads as the shells began to retaliate against our invisible enemy, began to grow more and more frequent, until the air was so full of them that it was the only thing that could encompass my thoughts.

I hated the Germans, more than I ever had done before; they had killed a lot of my friends and obliterated a great many more of my extended comrades. But still, as those shells rocketed their way towards wherever they were hiding, I couldn't help but feel sorry for them.

No one deserved to be on the end of a barrage such as that one, the blackened sky above us owing to the sheer amount of ordnance that ripped through the clouds and descended upon them like vultures.

In between the shrieking of artillery shells, I thought I could make someone out shouting. Looking over at Bob, he had heard it too and was already making moves to begin stubbing his cigarette out on the trench floor, to go with all the other stubs that we had tossed down there over the last hour or so.

After a while and a few more shrieks of artillery, a captain, one that I had never seen before, but who had clearly been in the advance, appeared from around the corner of the trench.

His arm was in a sling, the dirtied piece of cloth that was keeping his arm up stained with a large roundel of blood just below his elbow.

He copped both Bob and me sitting there, and began to announce to the whole trench, above the din, what must have been our first orders from an officer since five o'clock this morning.

"All walking wounded are to fall back. We're going back to our original lines. You'll meet up with reinforcements there to expect a German counter attack. From there you can await your orders from your respective regiments."

I sighed as I looked across at Bob, who already had two ciggies poking from his lips as he lit them. He shrugged at me as he passed me one, raising his eyebrows theatrically.

"What can you do?" he declared, almost chipperly, as if he had put the events of the morning behind him already.

Nothing. There was nothing we could do. We had always been cannon fodder, and I was certain that this war would carry on until not a single man was left alive on this continent.

Reaching to my top pocket I pulled out Sergeant Needs' flask. I turned it over a few times in my palm, before sipping at the very final remnants of the paraffin that was within.

I had lost all my hope. I would die here and for the

first time as I thought about it, nothing stirred in the pit of my stomach. Nothing at all.

I smirked to myself as I popped the flask back in my pocket, determining that it would go with me wherever I went in the remainder of my war.

"What you smiling at?" Bob piped up, as we heaved ourselves from our makeshift seats and prepared to move away from the trench.

"I was just wondering if anyone in the regiment was still alive for us to take orders off, that's all."

THE END
Follow Andrew Ellis as he continues to fight on the Western Front in 'Wavering Warrior' available on Amazon now!

GET A FREE BOOK TODAY

If you enjoyed this book, why not pick up another one, completely free?

'Enemy Held Territory' follows Special Operations Executive Agent, Maurice Dumont as he inspects the defences at the bridges at Ranville and Benouville. Fast paced and exciting, this Second World War thriller is one you won't want to miss!

Simply go to:

www.ThomasWoodBooks.com/free-book
To sign up!

YOU CAN HELP MAKE A DIFFERENCE

Reviews are one of my most powerful weapons in generating attention for my books.
Unfortunately, I do not have a blockbuster budget when it comes to advertising but
Thanks to you I have something better than that.

Honest reviews of my books helps to grab the attention of other readers so, even if you have one minute, I would be incredibly grateful if you could leave me a review on whichever Amazon store suits you.

Thank you so much.

ABOUT THE AUTHOR

Thomas Wood is the author of the 'Gliders over Normandy' series, Trench Raiders as well as the upcoming series surrounding Lieutenant Alfie Lewis, a young Royal Tank Regiment officer in 1940s France.

He posts regular updates on his website
www.ThomasWoodBooks.com

and is also contactable by email at
ThomasWoodBooks@outlook.com

twitter.com/thomaswoodbooks
facebook.com/thomaswoodbooks

Printed in Great Britain
by Amazon